JEWS
VS
ALIENS

First published 2015 by Jurassic London
First standalone print edition published 2016 by Ben Yehuda Press
www.BenYehudaPress.com

ISBN-13: 978-1-934730-62-1

Cover by Sarah Anne Langton
www.secretarcticbase.com

eBook conversion by handebooks.co.uk

20170205

JEWS VS ALIENS

Edited by
Rebecca Levene &
Lavie Tidhar

CONTENTS

INTRODUCTION

The alien in science fiction, it is often said, stands in for the Other in all its myriad forms. I like to think sometimes a four-armed Martian warrior is just a four-armed Martian warrior, as Freud would have said, but the point stands. The legendary Golden Age editor, John W. Campbell Jr., famously objected to authors' use of their overtly-Jewish names, suggesting a pseudonym — because "the readers won't like it". Isaac Asimov got away with it (his first short story was already published in a non-Campbell magazine) but well recalled Campbell's gentle conviction of the superiority of the white Nordic male. Indeed, the reason there are no aliens in Asimov's Foundation trilogy is due to Campbell's editorial demands that aliens be presented as inferior to humanity.

To Campbell, of course, the Jews were the aliens — but what happens when the roles are reversed? Rebecca Levene and I have asked a group of today's writers to tell us. Appropriately, they come from across the Jewish Diaspora — from the United States and Israel, the former USSR, Australia and England — and I hope their responses delight you as much as they have us.

In the tradition of Tzedakah, all money earned will be donated to charity. You can read about our chosen charity in About The Charity at the end. I'd like to thank my co-editor, Rebecca, our publisher, Jared, and all our writers, for making this little book possible. If you enjoy it, you might care to check its companion volume, Jews vs Zombies, since we couldn't resist doing both!

Lavie Tidhar
2015

ANTAIUS FLOATING IN THE HEAVENS AMONG THE STARS

ANDREA PHILLIPS

A glossy holobrochure on very fine, super-heavyweight haptic sheeting. Fabricated with remarkably high (and visibly expensive) production values.

Welcome to Antaius Floating in the Heavens Among the Stars, the galaxy's premiere spot for luxurious accommodation, fine dining, and views so beautiful they are capable of halting your autonomous biological functions temporarily!

We will unquestioningly conform to every physically possible detail and notion you request from us in writing, no matter your species or individual tastes.

- Festive and Sombre Cultural Celebrations
- Public Mating Rituals
- Status-Acquiring Occasions
- Propaganda Assemblies
- Corporate Events

Sublimate Your Guests With Luxury at Antaius Floating in the Heavens Among the Stars

Our sweeping views of the burning heart of the galaxy as it destroys itself are sure to make your antennae quiver with self-abnegation, superstitious fervour, and romance! But the luxury does not stop with astronomical features detectable from our location. We also have extensive internal luxurious accommodation available!

At Antaius Floating in the Heavens Among the Stars, our decor is specified and executed on a case-by-case for each event that we contractually host. Icefalls, slime baths, neuroreactive lighting, olfactory gardens, intoxicant clouds, conductive netting — make a wish and we will generate it!

If you are the outdoorsy type, we can obtain botanical and non-sentient life from any planet and in any stage of development to replicate a specific ecosystem. If your tastes run to nanoplatinum sheeting and electrocrystal matrices, this also can be created!

Comfort That Cannot Be Compared to Other Comforts You May Be Familiar With

We are fully knowledgeable regarding the diverse variety of customs, preferences, and physical requirements of every sentient species recorded in the K6-nn?%n9A Guide to Galactic Life. With our team of xenologists, exobiologists, and cyber-hybrid maintenance and waitstaff, you may rest easy knowing that every molecule you respire and ingest will not only be uncontaminated by potentially fatal microtoxins and disease agents... it will also be completely enjoyable to all of your pertinent sensory apparatus!

Please note that some types of accommodation may incur additional fees, including but not limited to events requiring an atmosphere over 0.38% hydrochloric acid, pressures exceeding 823 kPa, or contraband items in violation of the Frou!ah!hehoa-Smith-Lllrwykp Treaty.

Sent via interpost:

My Darling Rachel,

Mazel tov on your happy news! Now that you're going to be taking care of my little Michael, I just wanted to make sure you're absolutely clear on all of his preferences for the wedding so you can make sure he has everything he needs on his happy day. Consider it my little gift to my new daughter!

First, did you make sure you can get real champagne and caviar imported all that way? Michael prefers top quality, even if it takes a little more work. And I'm sure you know to get no roses for the chuppah, and no soy on the menu at all. Michael has always been allergic and the last thing you need is for him to wheeze and swell up on your wedding night. Oh, and you really must include those little cocktail franks during the cocktail hour. I know they're not the most highbrow thing, but they are his absolute favourite, so you simply must have them. Boys will be boys!

One more thing — you remember that our Uncle David is a rabbi and his family are very, very frum, of course? You know I don't care one way or the other if the wedding is kosher or who sits where, I'm very easy to please, but the way you put on your affair is going to have certain implications for how the family receives you.

Love and kisses!
Your New Mum

Printed in an ornate script on old-fashioned creamy vellum card stock:

Hors D'oeuvres
Crudités with olives and pickles
Skewered fruits from the Seven Systems
Caviar and smoked salmon three ways
Roasted game fowl
Oxygen bar
Pigs in blankets

First Course
Salad of crisp Ooolovoba seaweed with citrus and puffed hazelnut

Main Course
Chateaubriand with flamed Velgan whiskey demiglace
Baby lamb chop with rosemary mist
Lentil patty with curry-raisin broth

Whipped potato with three toppings
Mirepoix spears

Dessert
Five-layer wedding cake with chocolate-cinnamon frosting
Gemmalian iceplum sorbet (sugar-free)

Sent via interpost:

Dear Rachel,

You know I'm not a complainer and I hate to complain, but I have to tell you that ever since you told me you're holding a wedding at that place run by those awful aliens, I just haven't been able to sleep at night. Are you sure this place is safe? Can they even put on a nice affair? Have they ever done something for humans before?

They say it's just like holding an event for the Loofpahrigas, but I don't believe it for a second. And I'm absolutely sure those tentacle-faced bags of swamp gas don't keep kosher! I'm not saying you have to put on a kosher wedding, you know I'm not picky and I don't care one way or the other, but as I've mentioned, some of the family are very observant.

Mazel Tov,

Edith

There is a hand-written message at the bottom:

Just ignore her, honey. I'll call tonight and handle this myself.

— M

An officially certified letter delivered via interpost, heavy with legal witness stamps and seals:

To Whom This May Concern:

As mentioned during our final tasting event last night at Antaius Floating in the Heavens Among the Stars, we have a lot of concerns about our upcoming wedding and the way that you plan to handle it. I know there have been some personnel changes since you hosted the completely lovely Bank of United Centauri end-of-fiscal-year party last year, but that is no excuse at all. The degree of incompetence you have displayed is nothing short of shocking.

First off, that 'lingering trace amount of methane' is beyond revolting and you have to get rid of it entirely. Zero methane, do you understand me? I don't care what you say is an acceptable concentration for oxygen-based atmospheres, it's just disgusting and we won't tolerate it.

The decorations were also completely lacking in taste. This is indeed a 'mating ritual', but that DOES NOT mean we want decorations shaped like human genitalia! It was positively vulgar, not to mention embarrassing, and I'm absolutely sure my future mother-in-law will never forgive me for this. I'm attaching several holograms from other weddings to this missive to make absolutely sure you know what we consider appropriate to the occasion.

The menu was also completely, catastrophically wrong. I understand that your offerings are 'perfectly nutritive' and won't kill human beings, but that doesn't mean we WANT to eat things from the oceans of Europa that look like nightmares, or desserts garnished with Trbillleagh tree-slime. It may be exotic and fashionable to be adventurous with alien intoxicants in some circles, but it is not to our taste, not in our contract, and there is no way we're paying for it.

The cake was better. At least it seemed to be actual cake, but the frosting should NOT be lentil paste. That is NOT EVER an acceptable substitute for chocolate. And where were the pigs in blankets, the puffed hazelnuts, or the lentil patties, I ask you? It's like you didn't even look at the menu we agreed upon!

It is also imperative that everything be kosher, which I gravely doubt was the case yesterday! Your services are not cheap, so if you don't know how to do a kosher meal yourself, I'm paying you enough money to hire a rabbi to certify everything on the spot. You said you could when we asked. Don't think for a millisecond we won't be holding you to your commitments.

With the wedding coming up in just 3.8 spins, we don't have time to break the contract and book a different venue, or reissue invitations so our guests can rearrange their travel plans. But I'm telling you now, if you don't get every detail right on the day of my wedding, we're taking you straight to court.

Respectfully Yours,
Rachel Cohen

An internal document from the Galactic-Class Discreet and Attentive Luxury Hospitality Hive Mind #1005587, proprietors of Antaius Floating in the Heavens Among the Stars:

Problem: Client #4487J-Cohen-Halevi/mating ritual expresses emotional dissatisfaction with physical demonstration of mating ritual service offerings, despite high-quality luxury offerings in line with legally binding written agreement of service.

Suggestion: Examine Client #4487J-Cohen-Halevi/mating ritual written report of emotional dissatisfaction carefully for actionable items to improve service offering in line with expectations.

Observation: Client #4487J-Cohen-Halevi/mating ritual speaks favourably of a prior experience with Antaius Floating in the Heavens Among the Stars.

Observation: Client #4487J-Cohen-Halevi/mating ritual assumes we possess a high degree of familiarity with species-specific trivia due to prior favourable experience.

Observation: Such knowledge was once available but is now unavailable since dissolution of our union with former member Harry Locantore.

Concern: No species expert compatible with Client #4487J-Cohen-Halevi/mating ritual is available at this time.

Suggestion: Cancel contract.

Concern: Potential legal liability for unexpected disruption of time-sensitive mating ritual.

Concern: Reputation of Antaius Floating in the Heavens Among the Stars may suffer more than 2.08% threshold for tolerable quantities of negative reputation should dissatisfied client testimony emerge.

Resolved: Reputation of Antaius Floating in the Heavens Among the Stars and Galactic-Class Discreet and Attentive Luxury Hospitality Hive Mind #1005587 are business objectives more important than other objectives with lesser priorities.

Resolved: Excellent service must be delivered to Client #4487J-Cohen-Halevi/mating ritual. Proceed with intensive independent research into species-specific environment, mating habits, and taboos in order to deliver a service in line with existing positive reputation.

Concern: Such research may be costly to such an extent that it surpasses the price agreed upon in the legally binding written agreement of service.

Resolved: Profit is a lesser objective in the situation involving Client #4487J-Cohen-Halevi/mating ritual, because reputation of Antaius Floating in the Heavens Among the Stars and Galactic-Class Discreet and Attentive Luxury Hospitality Hive Mind #1005587 are higher priorities determining future course of business as a whole.

Observation: Client #4487J-Cohen-Halevi/mating ritual is of species subtype Sol-Human-Spacebound-Cis/Het-Jew.

Observation: Reference materials indicate species subtype is a 91.98% match with major traditions and physiology of Wazn-Beehao-Spacebound-Flex/Ase-Wruachh.

Observation: New applicant to join the hive named Eeeshee-5998 has documented in job application total fluency with major traditions and physiology of Wazn-Beehao-Spacebound-Flex/Ase-Wruachh.

Suggestion: Hire new applicant and conduct mating ritual in accordance with practices suggested by new species subject matter expert, thus saving money and providing excellent service compatible with existing positive reputation.

Resolved: Hire applicant. Proceed with mating ritual.

A news article in The New Singapore Chronicle:

Bride Sees Red Over Live Pigs

The new Mrs. Rachel Cohen-Halevi is suing posh restaurateur and event manager Antaius Floating in the Heavens Among the Stars after what she claims to be a poorly orchestrated wedding that 'completely ruined my day and set a dark cloud over my new married life.'

Chief among her complaints: 'When I asked for pigs in blankets, I certainly didn't mean actual live pigs wrapped in flannels! Even the poorest xenosociologist on their staff should have known better.' Cohen-Halevi claims that the presence of these swine was unsanitary and in violation of food safety standards, an affront to her religious beliefs, and 'made our whole wedding seem like a trashy joke'.

Antaius Floating in the Heavens Among the Stars defended its service vehemently. The hive issued a statement reading in part, 'The customer's requests were unreasonably unspecific and we cannot be blamed for any failures resulting from her own lack of communication with us regarding her specific preferences.'

Cohen-Halevi is suing for *3.7 billion in reparations for mental cruelty plus punitive fines for another *18 billion.

Sent via interpost:

Rachel,

For obvious reasons, the family isn't comfortable with coming to you for seder this year. We expect Michael will be joining us at home, naturally.

As for you, I don't want to say you're not welcome, of course you're welcome, but we think it might be better for everyone if you celebrate on your own this year. Do have a lovely holiday!

Best!

Edith

THE MATTER OF MEROZ

MEROZ

ROSANNE RABINOWITZ

Samuel's mind is ablaze from tzaddik Avrom's lecture.

He nudges his friend Lev. 'Bet they didn't teach about that at yeshiva!'

An old fellow in the front row turns around to glower at the boys. Then with a fury of phlegmatic throat-clearing he opens the discussion.

'Tzaddik, will you explain just how beings from other worlds could have souls? Hashem bestowed the Torah on Man. There is only one Torah as there is only God. And we are the only creatures who have been granted free will by Hashem.'

The tzaddik counters: 'But each congregation has its own Torah, so why shouldn't each world have its version of the sacred scrolls?'

He runs his fingers through his ginger and grey beard as he thinks. 'Look at the Book of Judges, where the prophetess Deborah curses the inhabitants of a place called Meroz for not helping the Israelites fight the Canaanite general Sisera. But where is a place called Meroz? No one knows, though there are references to stars. So the Talmud concludes that Meroz must be a star or planet. So wouldn't this curse recognise that the inhabitants of Meroz have the ability to think, to choose between good and evil?'

'But...' Samuel starts. Everyone turns to look at him and he wants to shrivel to a speck of dirt on the floor. How dare he, a smooth-faced outsider, speak up?

The tzaddik smiles and nods at him.

He clears his throat. 'So how can someone from our world curse those who live upon another world? How does a curse travel over such a long distance?'

'If a curse punishes the ungodly, surely Hashem makes the curse effective,' comments the surly denizen of the front row. 'Do you doubt the power of the Lord?'

'No, Dov. This young man asks a good question,' says the tzaddik. 'Yes, the Almighty is the supreme power in the universe. He has also endowed his favoured creatures with free will and a capacity to overcome physical obstacles, such as vast distances. For example, Rashi explains how the road folded itself up for Jacob when he travelled from Beersheba to Haran, so he was able to complete his journeys in an instant. This manner of travel is described as the leaping of the road, kefitzat haderech.'

'What did he say about a road?' Lev whispers to Samuel.

'Shush!'

'Deborah and other adepts could make the roads "leap", thus shortening the distance they had to travel between two places. They could also instigate the crumpling of the sky, which allows travel between the stars. Then they made the sky smooth again and restored the distances.'

He's never read that in the Talmud. Maybe he missed something. 'Where do you learn how to do these things?' he asks.

Now the tzaddik frowns. 'This isn't something to do in your home! It is dangerous, and it is forbidden.'

'But you're telling everyone about it. How forbidden is that?'

'My son, it is one thing to know about this. It is our history, our birthright. But to know how to do this...' The tzaddik shakes his head. 'This knowledge is handed down to one person in each generation. There may be a time when we have to use it. But that time isn't now.'

It hurts Samuel's head to imagine that such things could be true. But it's a pleasant ache, like the one he gets when he tries to imagine the 'unseen colours' from his favourite section in the Zohar: 'There are colours that are seen, and colours that are not seen.' When he walks around the village, and the mud is grey and brown beneath his feet, he imagines those unseen colours, dazzling behind the muck. And what unknown colour lurks behind the dreary ledgers at the tailors' shop where he works? He hopes to discover it some day.

After more discussion, the tzaddik calls a halt. 'Now it is time to dance.' He gestures and the klezmorim take their places on the platform.

They begin their tune, slowly. Samuel stays in his seat next to Lev.

He remembers warnings that the Hasidim seek to convert other Jews. Though he enjoyed the discussion, he has no intention of joining their sect.

Soon wine is passed to Samuel and Lev. They drink and clink glasses, and the music is too catchy. They just have to join in. Legs kicking, the boys clasp hands on each other's shoulders, song vibrating in their throats and raising their lips.

In the dancing, Samuel feels his heart expand until it becomes a much greater heart that beats at the centre of the universe.

The two boys head home across the fields, a good hour's walk. 'I wish the road could rise up to meet us now,' Samuel says.

'Your head's more likely to hit it first, after all the wine you drank,' answers Lev.

'No, my eyes are on the stars!' Samuel giggles.

'But the tzaddik didn't talk about golems,' Lev goes on to kvetch. 'I was hoping for advice on that. I still don't understand why our formula hasn't worked.'

'Feh! Golem, shmolem… Your mind's in the mud — look at the sky instead!'

It's a clear night, and the stars are hypnotic. So many and so far, they appear as mist across the heavens. And each of them surrounded by worlds! Samuel reaches up to the sky, reaching out with spread fingers then closing his hand into a fist. Is this how you crumple the sky? But there is nothing in his hand.

'Samuel? Look where you're going!'

Drek. A huge cowpat.

Samuel wipes his boot on the grass.

Lev watches. 'A fitting end to the evening,' he observes. 'The tzaddik did say some interesting things. And these Hassidim enjoy a dance and so do I. But what's the point of dancing if there are no girls?'

Samuel swipes his boot one last time. 'You sound like my meshugge socialist sister, though she would ask that question for different reasons.'

And now his crazy sister will be coming home from Odessa.

Raizl swings a suitcase in each hand. Samuel is supposed to meet her train, but where is he? Maybe it's just as well she didn't bring her favourite weapon, the pole with spikes. She would have wrapped it in burlap and schlepped it here along with her two suitcases filled with schmattes, but Arkady talked her out of it.

However, she did bring her revolver. After the last pogrom in Odessa, trouble is expected everywhere, even in sleepy old Fekedynka.

At least there's a newly formed group of comrades here. She looks forward to meeting them. She's brought them a gift from her group — a megaphone. But she really ought to try it out first and make sure it works.

25

She holds her head high, sure she is observed. Here comes the Odessa mama! Back home, are you? Still not married? Of course not.

Home. The place where she was born stopped being home long before she left it at fourteen. She's only just off the train and already she misses Arkady. She misses Odessa, though not all its memories are good.

Drying pools of blood in the first rays of sun. She catches her breath. A memory. It's only a memory. This village doesn't even have gutters, only dirt roads.

'Raizl!'

So now Samuel is here. 'What time do you call this, schmattekopf? Never mind, don't worry about helping me with my luggage. I'm a strong girl.'

'Ah, Raizl, I see you haven't changed.'

'Why should I?'

In the deepening dusk crows rise from the fields, flying over the village. It has spread out since she was last here, two yeas ago when her father died. Now it's almost a town.

As they walk, Raizl hears the Odessa-bound train pulling into the station, then letting out a blast of its whistle as it leaves. A part of her wants to be on it.

When they arrive, Raizl's mother Feygele emerges from her last-minute packing, preparing for her journey to Vilna to live with her eldest daughter.

She actually looks younger than last time; it must be anticipation of the new life and the growing brood of grandchildren awaiting her. She's got rid of her sheitel and has let her own hair grow again, lightly covered by a scarf. Raizl is glad for her choice of present, a lovely embroidered scarf from Smyrna. Mother doesn't have to know that it fell off a boat in Odessa harbour and into Raizl's hands before it hit the water.

Feygele brings out the samovar, along with a plate of rugelach. Raizl has fond memories of those buttery bites tasting of nuts, raisins and cinnamon. But they are dry in her mouth now.

Siblings, relatives and neighbours drop by to bid Feygele goodbye. Some glare at Raizl, the wayward daughter packed off to the Odessa cousins. Raizl smiles back. She doesn't care what they think.

Sister Hannah and her husband arrive with their twins. Those warm milky bundles are quickly parked on Raizl's lap, one on each thigh.

She does like babies, provided they aren't her own.

Once the guests depart, the table is cleared and Feygele retired, Raizl takes a bottle of vodka out of her bag and pours two generous portions.

'You're better off with this than the kosher wine, Samuel.' They raise their glasses to each other, then knock back their drinks.

Raizl clears her throat. 'So, Samuel… You know that mother wouldn't leave unless I promised to "look after" you. So I'll tell you now what that means. I'm here if you need me, but I won't be your servant. In Odessa, living with my comrades, we eat and cook together and share all tasks. That's what will happen here.'

'But… I have to work and study.'

'So will I. How do you think we'll eat?'

'I can't cook. And everyone will laugh.'

'Ha! Let "everyone" learn to cook too! You don't do your part, I go on strike. But maybe you'll see sense with more vodka. And what do you study, which is so important that you can't cook a meal?'

Samuel looks away from Raizl. 'Kabbalah, that's what we study. Me and Lev. Lev shares his yeshiva books, but we go our own way with them.'

'Oy Samuel. You once wanted to learn science. You liked to learn about animals and plants and look at the stars. So what's this?'

'But I still look at the stars. We went to a lecture about them by a tzaddik. He believes that beings from other worlds have visited the earth. It's in the Talmud.'

'So if it's in the Talmud, does that make it true? A smart boy like you, believing in bupkes,' Raizl says. 'And what are these other worlds? Mars? I read a book about an invasion from Mars. War of the Worlds. In English. I've been studying English at a workers' institute and they had it in the library. The librarian told me that H.G. Wells is an important socialist and this is a book about the British class struggle!'

Samuel snorts. 'I've never heard of it.'

'It's just a story. Our librarian doesn't know English. My English wasn't so good then, but I improved it by reading this book. I might try to find pupils for English here.'

'Most people here don't even speak Russian.'

She shrugs. 'So I teach Russian. Even here in Fekedynka the new twentieth century starts! Parents will want more for their children than superstitious chazzerai from the cheder.'

Raizl pours herself another vodka. 'But you know, farshtunken Fekedynka is still a miserable excuse for a village. You should come back to Odessa with me. Even with the quotas against Jews, you can study with your circle of friends, then pass your exams. You can become a scientist. My friend Leah...'

Raizl stops. When the pogrom started, comrades divided into groups to defend certain areas. It was only by chance Leah ended up in the group that met with a massacre. Raizl had originally volunteered for that group, then Leah said she preferred it because she had family in that area.

Raizl shudders with guilt for surviving, sorrow for the friend she lost.

Samuel is waiting for her to finish the sentence.

'My friend studied science. But she was killed.'

'So you want me to go there and get killed too? What a great sister you are!'

'Yes, it's dangerous in Odessa. But it's dangerous everywhere. All it takes is one incident, one accusation... Maybe you need to look up from your books and your crazy Kabbalah davening.'

'You call me crazy but anyone might say the same thing about you.'

Maybe I am, Raizl thinks. She knows she should lie low, when revolutionaries and activists in the self-defence groups are likely to face arrest. But how low can she lie if the trouble comes here? She's already been invited to speak to the local comrades and help with their self-defence practice.

'So, Raizl, how's it going with your shaygetz, your Russian fancy-boy?' Samuel lowers his voice, even though he can hear their mother snoring above their heads.

They both raise their eyes to the ceiling, and Raizl answers in an even lower voice. 'Arkady? As well as expected. I hope you'll meet him one day.'

They drink a last glass of vodka. The conversation lightens, turning to visits from the matchmaker and tips on foiling plans for unwanted marriages.

Finally, it's time to sleep. Samuel goes up to his room, while Raizl takes the pallet down and covers it with blankets. She undresses and stretches out, still warm with the heat from the fire left burning in the grate.

Raizl drifts into sleep. She sees flames and desolation, a home levelled to rubble. A tree-lined street near the sea, glittering glass on the road and blood drying in puddles.

Samuel and Lev make their way across the fields on Sunday afternoon, hoping they can talk to the tzaddik on his own in the study house.

'This tzaddik is meshugge for the stars and he's not much good on golems. But I like him after all,' says Lev. 'More fun than our rebbe, eh?'

'I told Raizl about him, but she said go to Odessa and learn real science.'

'What does she know? She hasn't heard Avrom. And women wouldn't be allowed in such a meeting.'

'They can study science, though. Raizl's friend in Odessa did.'

The one who was killed, Samuel reminds himself.

'So,' says Lev. 'That doesn't say much for science!'

They stop at some woodland near a stream, planning to relieve themselves before moving on.

Samuel undoes his trousers. While he attends to his business he closes his eyes as he recites a prayer. Commentators in the Midrash spoke of becoming close to God during the most humble activities. They said nothing about activities as humble as this, but shouldn't they be celebrated? To take in nourishment and excrete it is part of living, Hashem's plan.

When he opens his eyes, he notices a dark shape on the other side of the stream. A touch of white to the indistinct darkness of the shape, a little blue?

He steps over the stones, across the stream to investigate. As he comes closer, a turbulent hollow in the pit of his stomach tells him what his eyes still refuse to see. A pale hand, blue and white fringed cloth, a tallis.

The tallis is covering the man's face. Samuel reaches out, lifting it away to reveal bruise-coloured skin, bulging eyes. Hair and beard, red and white.

The tzaddik.

Samuel screams.

His friends run over. At the sight of the tzaddik, Lev joins Samuel's lamentation.

'We have to go tell them,' Lev finally says.

'Go. I'll stay with the tzaddik.'

'You can't stay. It isn't safe. What if...'

'What if? We can't leave the tzaddik's body alone. Go!'

Lev doesn't argue again, seeing Samuel's determination.

Now that he's alone with the tzaddik, Samuel pulls up the tallis to cover the dead man's face, this time with reverence. He sees the dark straps bound tight around his throat. The man was strangled with his own tefillin.

Samuel falls back as if this horror has just punched him in the gut. His hand thrusts into leaves, touches a soft fabric. He finds a square velvet bag. It is a plain deep green, worn in places.

Inside he finds a brass cylinder with four retractable sections, leather covering the largest section. A telescope, an instrument for looking at the sky!

There is also a book, a very old one. There's no title on the cover so he has to look inside. The Book of Deborah — the prophetess Deborah who could make the sky fold and crumple.

He says a kaddish for the tzaddik while clasping the book and telescope tight in his hands.

He hears shouts, people responding to the alarm raised by his friends. Who will come? The Hasidic burial society, the tzaddik's students, or the police? Hey hey daloy politsey, as his sister used to sing over the washing. Down with the police, down with the Czar. A better tune than that dirge she used to sing, all about being hated and driven away. Of course you'll be hated and driven away if you sing that drek.

He puts the precious objects back into the velvet bag and slips it under his shirt, under his tallis, and waits.

When Raizl was growing up in this village, she believed she was alone in her desire for a better world. There were rich people, and poor people. Among the poor people you found poor Russians, and poor Jews. The two groups fought each other more than those who kept them poor. She was only a child, but she knew this wasn't right.

And here in farshtunken Fekedynka, she is now meeting a small but active group affiliated to the General Jewish Labour Bund. There are fresh-faced gymnasium students from the better-off homes as well as youngsters from poor homes like hers. A few older people, like Mordecai the blacksmith. He says he joined after Jew-haters vandalised his smithy. His daughter, a sharp-face girl called Sheindl, had recruited him.

They are meeting in the woods for some short talks, then shooting practice. Though it's a chilly day, they are sheltered by the trees and the slope of the valley.

She'd been invited to talk about events in Odessa. But these now fill her with despair after all the hopes of a near-revolution — the strikes and rallies, crowds gathering at the harbour to support the Potemkin mutiny.

Being here makes her think of Arkady, though he obviously didn't attend Bund meetings. He had questioned the need for a separate group of Jewish activists, and they still argue about it. To her, it's practical when Jews often live and work separately from goyim, and even speak their own language. But Arkady's group of anarchists often worked with the Bund, helping especially with the self-defence.

So that's what they have to do now, defend themselves, rather than build a new world. It's a grim thought, yet these comrades lift Raizl's heart. These are boys and girls with dreams and hopes. She envies them for their confidence, something she lacked at their age. She'd been a shy girl, though she'd had moments of boldness.

She had heard about a boy in the village called Yankel who shared her views, and she just had to speak to him. He could become her soul mate, a true comrade… perhaps more. She decided to call on him to talk about their mutual interests.

When she knocked on his door, his mother opened it and Raizl explained that she wanted to meet her son. Yankel's mother slammed the door in Raizl's face. Later, she was denounced as a girl of loose morals and a disgrace to her family. But this led to a new life when she was sent off to stay with her cousins.

That same boy is here, asking her about Odessa.

'We've heard about your bravery in the revolution and fighting the pogromists,' says Yankel.

She's an Odessa mama again!

Revolution? It had only gone halfway.

Brave? Years ago, Raizl had been terrified just to knock on this young man's door. And how brave had she been in Odessa?

She remembers a Jewish woman with wild hair running up to their group, throwing a stone at their banner. At the time, they were marching in response to the Czar's reform manifesto. This woman didn't think they were brave.

'You bastards! They are chopping people up over there and here you are taking a little stroll. Your banners mean less than bupkes.'

So they rushed over to the woman's neighbourhood and stopped the attacks. They did save lives on that street. But they were too late or too few to stop other crimes.

A mother hung upside down by her legs, with the bodies of her six children arranged in a circle below.

A baby thrown out of a window.

It would've been much worse if we hadn't acted, Raizl tells herself.

Raizl tries to share what she knows, though it doesn't seem to be enough. She tells them that non-Jewish workers helped by forming self-defence groups and supporting pogrom victims. Railway workers, metal workers, sailors… But others? Maybe it was a worker who had thrown that baby out of the window.

Yankel says they have support from a socialist doctor called Oleg, plus other local activists. Some peasants are sympathetic, especially those who've been working or trading with Jewish families. But many others don't have these ties.

Then they get on to shooting practice. Only a few have guns. Some are very old: something a father kept from conscript days. A few have Bulldog guns like hers. No rifles or bayonets.

'A comrade from Odessa will try to bring more arms. In the meantime, we can practise with what we have. And remember, we do a lot with an iron pole, especially if our blacksmith modified it with spikes,' says Raizl.

Those who know how to shoot show the newer recruits, aiming first for the lower branches in trees. Yankel suggests the best thing for target practice would be a portrait of the Czar, but who would have such a thing?

Someone shoots a partridge. This is met with cheers. Then they begin shooting at other birds. There'll be a good meal after the practice, even if it's not kosher. matzo balls might not go well with partridge soup, but their catch should make a good stew.

Raizl concentrates on instructing the girls. She takes Sheindl aside, holds her arm and warns her to prepare for the recoil.

Then there's a crashing in the undergrowth.

Thank goodness no one has a jumpy trigger finger, because it's only Samuel.

'How did you know we were here?' She's pleased, thinking he wants to join them.

'We heard you! We're not deaf!'

Raizl nods, and introduces Samuel to her comrades. 'My brother.'

'The tzaddik is dead,' says Samuel. His eyes are red as if he's been crying. 'He's been murdered. And the Hasids were asking for all of you to guard the funeral.'

'Tzaddik Avrom only wanted to look at the stars. That's what the rebbe said. He went out walking to look at the stars, and they killed him.'

Raizl tries to console Samuel. She doesn't think she has anything left for that while she mourns Leah. But she is surprised how grief lightens when it is shared.

She is also surprised that the Hasidic community asked the Bund for help. Jewish elders usually petition the authorities for protection, but they must have seen indifference from the police when they reported the murder of an itinerant tzaddik.

Their group will stand guard outside the synagogue, then flank the procession to the cemetery.

The Bundists arrive well before the mourners with about forty in their group, including sympathisers from other parties. All have guns or poles, prepared for trouble.

A clot of people are already standing near the Hasidic synagogue. Raizl recognises a few faces. A local landowner, a horse merchant, some young labourers. All these people glare and swear when their group arrives.

But she catches nervous glances among the Jew-haters. Perhaps they don't expect resistance from Hasidic funeral-goers.

Could the murderer be among this crowd, or is he lurking further in the shadows?

'Mamzers,' mutters Sheindl. 'Surprised to see us, are they? Think we'll go like lambs to the slaughter...'

'Mamzers they are, but you don't shoot now,' says Raizl. She can see that Sheindl's on edge, her hand clutched around the gun in her pocket.

There's nudging from the other side, and one of them shouts out as if on a dare: 'What are you doing here? Not a beard among you. Are you Jews or just Jew lovers?'

Sheindl has to shout back: 'And what are you, if you have nothing better to do than hang around here?'

'I used to have a job but a Jew took it away.'

Now the mourners are arriving. They hesitate at the sight of the hostile bunch. A woman holds her hands up in supplication.

'Bugger off to Japan or Palestine!'

The Bundists surround the mourners, creating a protective corridor so they can file into the temple. Most of them weep. But Raizl is dry-eyed. She has no tears to spare for a man she's never met, but she will defend those who mourn him.

'One Jew down, too many to go.'

The man who calls that out gets too close and receives a warning poke with a pole. 'Think you're tough with your little sticks,' he sneers as he backs off. 'You won't do so well next time.'

But with the mourners all in the synagogue, the Jew-haters start to get bored and drift away.

The young Bundists grin at each other. By standing together, they've seen the trouble off. The funeral prayers wafting from the synagogue do little to dim their enthusiasm. Yisgadal, v'yisgadal... the mourners' kaddish.

Last time Raizl heard that was at her father's funeral.

Now the mourners file out of the temple with the coffin. Their Hasidic garments make a ribbon of black against the brown and grey fields, heading to the cemetery.

As they march out with the mourners, Raizl sees dark figures at the top of the hill. These are not the departing louts, but gentlemen who sit like officers on their horses. Watching. And waiting, she fears.

On her way home, Raizl watches Samuel and Lev disappear into the woods. The boys are up to something. She follows them.

'Hello, little brother. What are you doing?'

They react with shrugging and shuffling. Then Samuel replies, 'We're just talking. We know there's going to be trouble. We have to do something.'

'You should have joined our shooting practice.'

'But will a few more shooters hold off the Black Hundreds and their friends in the army? You said that yourself the other day,' argues Samuel.

For a kid whose head is filled with mystical nonsense, sometimes Samuel asks the right questions. The sad ones.

'So you are right. Like a broken clock. But what do you suggest?'

The three look at each other. 'We've only started to talk,' says Samuel.

'I know! We can raise a golem,' says Lev.

'A golem! Something out of fairy tales. Are you mad?'

'I think I've worked out what went wrong with our formula last year,' continues Lev.

'Last year indeed!' Samuel's contempt for the idea matches Raizl's. 'Golems! You are lost in the sixteenth century! What good is a man of clay and stone when our enemies can blow it up. Boom! We need more than a golem. And the answer could be in here.'

He pulls a book from out of the inner pocket of his coat. 'The Book of Deborah. I… found it on the ground near the tzaddik, along with a telescope.'

He looks around as if expecting condemnation. 'It was meant to be,' he adds.

'I don't know about what was meant and what was not. This book might be a lot of dreck.' says Raizl. 'But you did the right thing. The village police could have stolen it. You know what that schmuck of a constable is like.'

'This book is not dreck,' Samuel shouts. 'It contains the words of the prophetess Deborah, and her instructions on how to contact other worlds. These are worlds beyond Mars, beyond our own star. This is a world circling the star Meroz.'

'A curse on Meroz and all its inhabitants,' quotes Lev. 'Deborah cursed these creatures. So who needs them now?'

'And how will we bring them here?' Raizl considers War of the Worlds. 'And why? Maybe they won't be our friends. They could be worse than the Cossacks. Did you think of that?'

'No, no… Deborah cursed them for what they didn't do. They wouldn't help the Israelites, and she cursed them by closing the passage point. But in this book, she says she regretted this action. She believes there may be ways to stir them to action, and future generations might need to reopen the point of passage. She also believed it can be a source of knowledge.'

'So what's this "passage point"? Not an airship or flying machine?'

'No ships or machinery are involved, only the principles of "kefitzat haderech"', making the roads leap,' says Samuel. 'It creates the passageway that enables you to move from one place to another in an instant. Except it involves the sky, and bending the substance of space.'

'Pah!'

'It's like this.' Samuel takes off his tallis, spreads it on a rock and puts his fingers on it on either side of the rock. 'Think of this tallis as space, as the distance you need to travel. So you close the space like this…' He draws his fingers together, folding the material, until his fingertips are touching. 'The crumpling of the sky!'

'Very clever. So this book tells you how to do that? Can I see it?'

Samuel places the book in her hands.

It isn't very big. If it contained such extensive secrets, Deborah must have made her points quickly. Now, if only Marx had done the same.

Raizl opens it to pages of Hebrew. She knows a smattering of Hebrew from synagogue, but it's a 'sacred' language not meant for women. Hebrew was never a language of food, love, work and life for her. Yiddish is her mother tongue, her mame loshen.

But the Hebrew in this book would have been Deborah's mame loshen.

The illustrations in the book are simple line drawings, but they are striking. They compel her eyes to see something more than what's there. This book must have historical value, even if it's only a made-up story like War of the Worlds.

Raizl tries to keep an open mind as they prepare. Ritual has its place for unbelievers as well as the devout. After Bund meetings, they link arms and sing 'In Struggle', 'The Oath' and the 'Internationale'.

And of course, they have a meal.

The boys take turns reading from Deborah's book.

There are other worlds around other stars, but this is the only path I was able to open. It may be due to the celestial creatures' nature, and ours. Perhaps the other worlds cannot be reached for good reasons.

I say 'celestial' and not 'divine'. Celestial pertains to the stars and the sky. They are part of the natural order made by our creator; they do not stand above it.

'Creator?' Raizl interrupts. 'There is no creator.'

'Shut up,' says Samuel. 'Do you want to hear this or not?'

'This is why we don't allow women to take part in rituals,' says Lev, stroking his barely sprouted beard.

'Deborah was a woman,' Raizl points out.

'Raizl has a point, Lev. Deborah was a woman. She communicated with celestial beings and had the power to open and close the gate to them.'

'Your sister is no prophetess,' argues Lev.

'You bet your tuches I'm not. And what's with 'prophecy' when we have 'free will'? How free can we be with some big zayde in the sky?'

Lev is about to retort when Samuel holds his hand up. 'Stop! We can discuss this later. This isn't a Talmudic talking shop, we need to plan something.'

A few lines in the Talmud, a secret book from a dead tzaddik. Yet scientists and socialists like Mr. Wells have also speculated about life beyond the earth.

So how do these other-worlders live? In these worlds, do some prosper while others grow poor? Do they have social and economic classes?

Now that makes sense, Raizl thinks. We will ask the workers from another planet to join in solidarity in our fight against the police, the Czar and pogromists.

'Let's do it,' says Raizl. 'But we do it along with other self-defence efforts.'

'Whatever you want, sister' says Samuel, as he opens the book to another section. 'This part is called "Preparing the Table". Now, Deborah says there are variations. There's a sequence that worked for her, but many things can affect the contact. She says these beings are volatile.'

'Volatile! Sounds like what we need,' says Raizl. 'So let's be clear: there's no fasting or mortifying our flesh? I won't be having that.'

'No fasting. No mortifying — only fortifying. But it's more than that. Deborah says "celestial sustenance" can connect the worlds.'

'Well, well, a universal nosh! But how do you know what these beings like? Deborah's people ate differently from us, I'm sure.'

'That doesn't matter. It's most important that the banquet is enjoyed by those who prepare it.'

'You mean it's me doing the preparing.'

The two boys look at each other and shuffle about in that abashed-boy way.

'But that's not how it will be,' Raizl insists. 'You'll have to make yourself useful in the kitchen. Both of you.'

Carrot tzimmes with honey and raisins, potato kugel and sweet noodle kugel. Hunks of barley bread to mop up the juices. Soup from the remains of Friday's chicken.

'You better get grating and chopping. Down to the knuckle, boys.'

'Ha, you're as bad as Chaim the tailor.'

'No, this is cooperative work. See, I get my hands dirty too, alongside you. And they're your guests anyway.

Raizl starts singing 'In Struggle', a favourite workers' anthem, as she mashes fish and crumbs together. 'We are the hated and driven, Tortured and persecuted, even to blood... 'Tis because we love the poor, The masses of mankind, who starve for food.'

Raizl chuckles to think she's preparing food while singing a song about the starving masses. But she's learned how to make a little go far: lots of matzo meal and seasoning. Short of revolution and expropriation, this helps fill the belly.

'We are shot down, and on the gallows hanged, Robbed of our lives and freedom without ruth — '

'Stop it!' Samuel complains. 'Yes, we all suffer. But do we have to suffer more? At least the Hasids play tunes that are good for dancing.'

'I'll think about changing the music after you do some work.'

Samuel shrugs, then closes the shutters.

'And what's that for? How do we make the sky crumple when we can't see it?'

Samuel opens Deborah's book and reads: 'The sky is space, and space is everywhere even when it is enclosed.'

'Space, schmace!' Raizl carries on with the preparations. But in keeping with the theme, she shapes the rugelach like stars.

When everything's bubbling on the stove, the boys spread a bed sheet out on the floor and begin drawing diagrams with charcoal and pens.

What are they doing to that sheet? These scholars will have to learn to do the washing too.

Samuel labels eight places at the table, and several in the middle. He adds lines around it, a vortex of rings around the centre, plus other figures.

'It's the Tree of Life,' says Samuel.

'Whatever you say, little brother.'

He draws lines linking the circles together, creating pathways and a central vortex. 'And the food goes here.'

So the table is set, and they place the food on the sheet following the symbols and geometrical figures from the Book of Deborah.

Finally, the rugelach is ready, warm and fragrant from the oven. Raizl hovers with the plate, then plonks it down on the trunk of the Tree of Life, in the centre.

'Tipheret!' exclaims Lev. 'It stands for beauty. And it's where the synthesis of opposites meet.'

'Well, it's where we find a plate of rugelach, our mother's best recipe. I put poppy seed in them and...'

The boys begin davening and genuflecting towards the food.

'Stop it. Eat!' orders Raizl as she picks up her knife and fork.

She is tasting every piece of gefilte fish she ever ate in this mouthful.

Then the carrot tsimmes is sweet and savoury at once. With nourishment of the chicken soup flowing into her veins, the symbols on their improvised tablecloth begin to make sense. That one there, under the plate of rugelach, does indeed look like an opening, a tunnel.

'Look, we've fortified ourselves. Now we carry on the ritual,' says Lev.

The boys start to chant what sounds like a series of numbers, pronounced in many languages as well as Hebrew. It puzzles Raizl. Singing the 'Internationale' might be a ritual too, but she knows what it means. It inspires her. But this?

'Raizl, you look confused. The chanting frees our awareness to travel and open the path,' says Samuel.

'So tell me, how do we chant and eat at the same time?'

'Stop with your squabbles,' interrupts Lev. 'We have a road to make rise, and a sky to crumple! Or have you two forgotten?'

'But I'm asking a perfectly good question.'

'So here's a perfectly good answer. The chanting is a kind of verbal alchemy. By forming these words, then changing its letters, we can change the nature of reality — or in our case, the distance between two worlds.'

'Alchemy, you say? So maybe food is an alchemy of the stomach. An alchemy of taste and scent as well as words and sound. They say the way to a man's heart is through his stomach.' How she hated that phrase when she was growing up. On the other hand, her home cooking did impress Arkady and all her comrades.

'So, boychiks, the way through the centre of the universe and out again is through the stomach too! What did Deborah have to say about that? Maybe we eat rugelach now, before you start making noise again.'

So Raizl eats a pastry crumb by crumb, the poppy seed, raisins and cinnamon lingering on her tongue. Then she starts on one she made with almonds and dates.

As the pile of rugelach on the plate diminishes, Samuel keeps rearranging the remaining pastries into a pattern. This pattern begins to make sense too. And then they begin chanting again. It starts a buzz in her ears, between her ears.

The pattern of pastries converges at Tipheret, a point of beauty and synthesis. She takes another, this one with sweet cheese curds and dried apricots from Odessa. A blaze of flavour at the point of her tongue, taking her far beyond Odessa. At the vortex of star-formed pastry is a tunnel, and there is something at the end of it. Light, colours rippling through an utterly new spectrum.

Other tunnels branch from the one they travel. Are there other worlds at each end? Maybe these are the worlds that will show solidarity. She takes a look...

It's only Fekedynka. But the dirt roads are paved, full of odd sleek automobiles.

At another tunnel she sees Fekedynka's synagogue in flames.

As a young girl she would have gladly burned that place down herself. Samuel would have no great love for it either after so many beatings at the cheder.

But this smoke fills the tunnel, catching in her throat and infecting her with fear. The fumes flood her with a taste of iron and meat. It makes her gag. Ominous outlines begin to reveal themselves through the smoke. A tower?

No no, leave this place…

She's afraid at first to look into other tunnels, but she hears music that tempts her. Like klezmer, though it's not very good. A fat man sings a song against a backdrop of a village like hers, while people wearing furs applaud.

She moves on to another tunnel lit by kaleidoscopic blocks of colour that warm her even more than chicken soup. The kaleidoscope turns to a living scene. Her farshtunken village again: but here's she's walking hand in hand with Arkady in the market. Everything is still lit by the colours of the kaleidoscope. She feels peace. She thinks she's happy.

But then a deep noise wells beneath her feet and wrenching bass vibrations churn her stomach and rattle her teeth, threatening to undo her. Shake her into pieces, breaking everything down…

'Raizl, stay with us!' A rough hand on her shoulder, Samuel shaking her. 'We bring them to us, you don't want to be going to them!'

The deep bass carries on, but now she feels anchored against it. Something shrill spills out of an opening in the floor along with it, a column of light that hurts her eyes, noise approaching melody.

The colours scream with the sound, and she has to close her eyes against them. Something breaks. Plates? The ceiling above her head? She grips Samuel's hand, and remembers how he once gripped hers when he was much smaller.

Then it's quiet. So quiet. And a strange man's voice addresses them in something that sounds like Hebrew.

Raizl opens her eyes. Two men and a woman sit at their 'table', clad in Arabian-style robes and sandals. It must be cold for them, even with the room warmed by cooking.

A lot of plates are broken, but someone has moved the rugelach aside. That plate is still intact and the leftover pastries have retained a somewhat shaken pattern.

Raizl takes a deep breath, picks up the rugelach and offers it to their guests.

These beings speak Hebrew, Samuel thinks. Not the devotional Hebrew he knows best. But it's close to the Hebrew of Deborah's book. One moment their old house was filled with eye-blasting light and colour and gut-wrenching noise. He forced himself to look, even if it shattered him.

These creatures are composed of noise, and they weave their unseen colours with it.

And now they sit here in robes and sandals, accepting Raizl's offer of rugelach.

Then in a blink they're wearing warm clothes too. They must have assembled the substance from the air, the vapours of the food, anything around them. From this they create their flesh and blood, their clothes. Some would consider them gods, but Samuel knows there are no other gods before Hashem. They are God's creatures just like he, his friends and his sister and the beasts of the field.

Yet jealousy stirs in his mind. Hashem created Man above all other creatures, yet here are creatures far more powerful. Perhaps the Lord was not pleased with what Man has become.

'We're speaking the right language?' The first word from the woman grates like a rusty hinge. Then the next one's soften. Each word makes her voice more like a woman's, a human that God created.

Samuel tries to stifle his envious and selfish thoughts. He answers, while his friends are still stunned, 'You're close. We use a similar language for prayer, and something else for every day.'

'Yiddish,' adds Raizl, still offering food. For all her revolutionary Odessa ways, Raizl can be so much like their mother. Perhaps he should become more like that too. In the end, he did enjoy the cooking.

'We tried to change to your form as soon as we entered, so we're sorry if we hurt your eyes and ears,' says one of the men at their table.

They're very polite for accursed inhabitants, thinks Samuel. But he can't bear to be polite himself. He needs to know so much.

What did they want with Earth and the ancient Israelites and why didn't they help? Samuel is not sure what to ask first.

The three new human-like beings look about. 'The stories we've heard of your world tell us of heat and light, and a very bossy woman,' says the woman.

'Have something to eat. You've travelled a long way. Rugelach isn't enough. We can talk later,' says Raizl.

'Eat?' one of the male aliens says.

The woman jabs him with her elbow. 'Food, remember? You put it in your mouth. That's the stuff that drew us here, where there are so many senses to experience.'

Raizl is thoughtful. 'Three strangers will attract attention in a village full of yentas. We need stories for them. Arkady can get papers. Our guests are students from the yeshiva, yes? And one of you is a sister of a student.'

'What is a sister?'

'A pain in the tuches, that's a sister,' replies Samuel. 'But my sister speaks sense when she says eat.'

So that's what they do. The alien woman takes a piece of gefilte fish with her fingers. After a small mouthful she seems to glow with pleasure in the food, as if a light has flickered on under her skin.

Lev clears his throat. 'It might be easier if you were all yeshiva students. Friends from a town not too close. But one of you will have to, um, change yourself, if you can do that.'

'I expect that will be me,' says the female. And then her face and form seems to melt. Now Samuel does look away. When he sees her again, she has become a brown-haired boy.

Remember, they are only creatures like me. They do things we cannot do. Maybe they can help us. But they are not God.

Finally he speaks up. 'Do you go around visiting other worlds?'

'When we can, though it's hard to get through. We need help from the other side. We like to sample things and study them. We create sound-scores to enjoy at home,' the first young man from space explains. 'Yours is the only world we've found where beings are so different from us, and produce such a wonderful and strange variety of sounds: some sweet, some harsh. We all heard stories about a visit, then access was denied. Some woman wanted us to fight in a war. We don't do wars.'

Samuel translates this into Yiddish for Raizl.

And Raizl answers, 'Neither do we, me and my comrades. Our only war is the class war — '

Lev interrupts, and soon they are talking about points and pathways and how these beings arrived. They pick up each other's Hebrew idioms quickly.

Raizl recognises some of the Hebrew words, but most of the time she watches. She sees how a light flickers in their faces as they enjoy their food.

The three look so ordinary now, but Raizl remembers the dazzle of their light and their pulsing waves of sound.

So these creatures of sound and light enjoy a vacation in the flesh. They change their size, they change their shape to look like us. They seem harmless, compared to the kind of humans she has dedicated herself to overturning.

They talk like people now. But she is sure she hears an echo in their voices, as if they come from across empty spaces. And their talk is empty too, empty of feeling.

It's like people going to the Black Sea to swim and eat ice creams. But this is no time to kibitz, no time to fool around. Not in Deborah's time when a wicked king held the Jews as slaves, and no time for kibitzing now.

So they want a vacation, they only want to schmooze and eat and drink and make 'sound-scores'. Raizl remembers what she saw at the end of a tunnel: the fat man singing on a stage, making an entertainment of someone's poor life.

They've assumed their bodies of flesh and blood for momentary pleasures, while that is all we have.

The three guests pick up their Yiddish quickly. Raizl puts them upstairs in the room she's taken over from her mother, so they'll be out of the way. She goes back to the pallet in the kitchen. It's warm there, and it's where she slept as a child.

If the visitors broke a few dishes on arrival, they are now the tidiest of guests. They've been given names: Hymie, Yaakov and Herschel.

They spend a lot of time in Samuel's room. She hears chanting and talking. They go out at night and look at the stars with the tzaddik's telescope.

45

Then they go to Odessa for a look around. It's just as well they're away, before they get a visit from the matchmaker urging them to marry someone's daughter.

When the guests return, they say how much they like Fekedynka. Especially the food. They're not so interested in fine things, but in strong tastes and aromas and sounds.

Raizl cooks another meal, more chicken soup for the schnorrers out of space.

Of course, she did try to get them to help in the kitchen. Yaakov-from-Meroz obliged. Not for him grating potatoes or any hard graft; he created something that looks very much like gefilte fish out of nothing, or 'emanations' as Samuel likes to say. But she didn't see anything emanating there, just some gefilte fish.

But then she took a bite. It tasted like damp sawdust. An imitation.

She remembers when she took Samuel on walks where they'd find flowers, collect them and look them up in a big book, their father's treasure. She should have tried harder to convince him to study this kind of science. He could have done something useful, instead of this...

Get rid of them, she's about to hiss at Samuel, who is now chopping onions. He has the book, he must know the curse to send them back. But she has also seen how the aliens flicker when something affects them. She remembers those bone-rattling notes, the unmaking chords at their heart. Surely the goniffs could be good for something. Even Deborah thought so.

Meanwhile, she tutors her pupils in Russian. At the end of it, a few coins. She goes to help sister Hannah with her babies, and tells her that Samuel has guests. Better say that, before the chitchat goes around.

Hannah has other concerns. 'There's been trouble,' she says. 'Drunk boys in the market mouthing off about a pogrom. They called it a cleansing, though they're dirty schmucks themselves. They were throwing rocks, while soldiers supplied vodka.'

On her way home, Raizl calls in on Mordecai. At his smithy the windows are boarded up and glass still glitters on the ground beneath them. He shows her a collection of spiked poles. Is that enough? Oleg said that he expects more arms to arrive, but they're overdue.

Raizl runs home. She goes up to Samuel's room, where the three guests would be. She flings the door open. 'Listen! Do you want to experience real life on this Earth? Soon you'll see it in all its horror. Life isn't just a bowl of chicken soup.'

They're all crowded around the open window. A cold wind blows through the room. Samuel turns around, holding his telescope. 'Ssh! They're showing me the stars with inhabited planets.'

Raizl is lost for a response. Then she goes downstairs and gets the megaphone she brought from Odessa. Time to try it out at last.

Back in Samuel's room, she shouts through it: 'Wake up, you schlubs!'

Alien guests and humans alike jump at the sound.

And maybe the creatures of sound and light jump a little more.

Doctor Oleg passes on the bad news. Comrades in Odessa have been arrested and arms were seized.

Faces of her friends flash before Raizl's eyes, but she doesn't have time to worry. Without these arms, they need other help. They knock on doors, get promises of a loan of a horse or cart. A few pistols are donated; the blacksmith will work overtime. They enlist the support of the Jewish toughs who hang about the market: these goniffs don't give a shit about politics but they'll pile in if a fight breaks out.

Raizl is at home, writing out a chart of Yiddish and Russian words. Then the blast of a shofar from the village synagogue interrupts her train of thought.

Since it isn't a holiday, that only means one thing.

It probably started in the market. It usually does. And that's where Raizl's group will go, while others patrol elsewhere.

Raizl shouts for Samuel, then gets herself ready. Heavy coat and scarf over her face, her stoutest pair of boots, her pistol in one hand and an iron stave in another. She picks up the megaphone and slings it across her chest with its strap. Though she doesn't expect to make speeches, they might need to communicate.

'And what are you going to do, boys?' Raizl turns towards Samuel and Lev. 'Cast some more spells?'

'No, we're going out! We'll defend the synagogue.'

She nods at her brother. 'There'll be a group heading there now. And where are your guests?'

'They went out to do some… recording, they called it.'

A curse on Meroz and all its inhabitants.

In Odessa, Raizl was able to dodge and run through the streets, shelter in buildings and alleys and emerge again.

But this is a village of ramshackle shops and dirt roads, exposed in a valley to an enemy that comes from all sides. From other villages, from the towns and even the cities, their enemies prepare to sweep through any place that stands after October's pogroms.

Some of these attackers are peasants, armed with pitchforks and scythes. But there are also soldiers among them, officers and Cossacks too.

She wants to vomit. Did Yankel speak of bravery? She'd flee if there was anywhere to go. The enemy will sweep them aside as easily as dust off a wooden floor, then go on to the next village.

She has her pistol. She'll take a few of them out of action, out of life before they kill her. But she doesn't want to die.

Then their guests appear in the crowd. Just behind her. Swathed in coats and scarves, like everyone else. Hymie, Yaakov and Herschel, the yeshiva boys from Meroz. They are pressed up close to her, and even though they just look like boys, it makes her shudder. They make noises to each other that bear no relation to a human language.

They don't write anything down, but they look at each other, look at the scene in front of them as if comparing notes.

Then there is a gunshot. Bayonets extended, swords and clubs raised, the Black Hundreds spill into the village.

There are screams from the front — are people getting trampled?

'Let's go,' Raizl shouts. 'We have to move forward.'

Pogromists come straight into the market, horsemen in front. Closer they come, then Raizl runs forward and shoots. The first horseman rears and falls. Yankel and Sheindl start a volley at the other horsemen, but not before other shots ring out.

Comrades scatter, but one ducks into the butcher's to emerge with a meat hook, showing a clear intention to use it.

The Bundists keep shooting, but in a flash they're surrounded and pushed back against the tavern. A Jewish thug called Mendel comes out of the tavern and starts throwing rocks. Someone starts shooting from the upstairs windows, just missing a Cossack but bringing down his horse.

But they're only a handful cornered here, plus the schnorrers out of space.

'A curse on Meroz!' Raizl echoes the prophetess Deborah.

She knows it's the end. She has chosen to live the life of a rebel, and she did the best she could. Now it's over but she'll make a good exit. She shoots and shoots. When she runs out of bullets, she's prepared to use a pole and then kick and punch if she loses that.

And she'll sing. This song will be the last thing in her ears, not the curses of the Black Hundreds. 'We are the hated and driven,' Raizl begins, lifting the megaphone to her lips.

Mordecai's bass voice booms out. Sheindl and Yankel, everyone joins in. 'Hated are we, and driven from our homes, Tortured and persecuted, even to blood; And wherefore? 'Tis because we love the poor....'

Yaakov-from-Meroz visibly shudders. Raizl can feel it move through him and convulse him. 'That... that... that terrible tune. Those words,' he complains in Yiddish, pulling his hat tighter over his ears. 'Farshtunken! Miserable!'

They sing louder. Then Raizl pulls his hat off, exposing his ears. 'Put that in your sound-score, you putz!'

Luminescence moves through his face, similar to the glow excited by the pleasure of good Jewish food. But now it expresses pain, shown by the way his too-human features contort. The light is stronger. And Raizl understands. Soon he will lose control, and stop being Yaakov.

Yes... Sound affects these creatures most, for that is what they are made of.

She sings through the megaphone. 'We are shot down, and on the gallows hanged, Robbed of our lives and freedom without ruth, Because for the enslaved and for the poor, We are demanding liberty and truth.'

The alien's body swells. And the other one gives a cry, worse than a fox in heat or a cat meeting its end.

'Sing louder, sing!' Raizl urges her friends. She kicks Mendel. 'Sing, goddammit!'

And Mendel sings.

The aliens burst out of their clothes; their flesh comes apart in shreds of light and patches of darkness.

The pogromists back off, frightened by what they see.

'But we will not be frightened from our path, By darksome prisons or by tyranny...'

The alien fleshly form dissolves into a tangle of waves that boom in pain, deep dissolving throbs that makes the horses bare their teeth, shriek and turn and bolt.

Meanwhile, other Jews emerge from defensive posts around the village. They move forward with sticks and guns ready to finish the job, even if they've had to share some of their enemy's pain.

Oleg and a few others tend to the injured on the ground.

Have the aliens fled, taking their sound-score with them? Maybe they've decided this world is not a suitable place for their holidays after all.

Or they could still be here in some form, lingering like the scent of a fish gone bad.

The tavern keeper emerges with flasks of wine. 'The mamzers have run away!'

Samuel and Lev arrive with others from the synagogue, followed by a beaming rebbe.

'It's God's doing, like the horns of Jericho,' intones the rebbe, accepting the offer of wine after a brief blessing.

But Raizl shakes her head and passes her wine to someone else. She remembers what she saw in the tunnel, the place where the sky crumpled and let in the alien light. Now she knows where Deborah's gift of prophecy came from. When she opened the pathway, those other corridors showed her what-could-be. Deborah did not predict the future, but she looked into possible futures.

Raizl can't forget the burning synagogue, the smoke that must hide a horror more brutal than any pogrom. But how will she speak of this to others? Who will listen? She understands now that Deborah might have been much more accursed than the inhabitants of Meroz. And so is she.

While the others toast and celebrate a victory, Raizl cannot join them.

ALIEN THOUGHTS

ERIC KAPLAN

The object had dropped from the sky and crashed into the forest behind the schul on Erev Shabbos. Schneerson, the doctor, had led a group of men to look at it, half buried in the dirt, a ring of luminous fungus around it glowing through the humus. A curse? the men he hired to dig it up wanted to know. A sign of a coming plague? A call us to repent? No, Schneerson had assured them, the earth is one of many bodies hanging in empty space, flying through darkness. Sometimes they jostle each other. Sometimes they knock each other. This was one such body that had gotten a knock in its home in the vastness and come crashing down behind the schul. God hadn't sent it.

'Take a look at this, doctor,' one of the men with shovels had said, standing up to his chest in the glass-lined pit the falling object had blasted in the forest floor.

Schneerson had jumped in, pushed him aside and inspected it. Carved in the black metal was a letter 'ה'.

The doctor ate pork on Yom Kippur, had electric lights in his home, drank coffee and played chess with gentiles and now he was hiking through the woods to see Reb Yaakov, the wonder rabbi. Schneerson and Yaakov had been friends in cheder. Schneerson always took care to hide it from his teachers when he knew more than they did; not so Yaakov. By six he had memorized the Torah, by eight the Talmud. By twelve he could tell you if you pricked Rashi with a pin, what letter would be on the other side. At his bar mitzvah, his rabbi had told him that more than intelligence, God valued a kind heart, and he had called him an ignoramus in front of the whole congregation. Now he lived in a one-room shack six hours into the woods. Children sometimes hiked out to see his emaciated form rolling naked in the snow, 27, 39, 106 times, and he screamed at them, wild as a demon, calling them idolaters, prostitutes and donkeys.

'Yaakov, it's Mendel.' The door opened. The rabbi was so emaciated,Schneerson could see the pulse in his neck. He has scurvy, the doctor thought. 'I thought you might be angry at me.'

'Because you eat pork? At least you're consistent.'

'Something strange has happened, Yaakov. An object fell from the sky. A meteorite.'

'So? Chazal discuss this. It is a piece of the dome the stars are in.'

'This was etched on the outside with letters as deep as my thumb.' Schneerson took the paper on which he had copied the letters and handed it to Yaakov.

The rabbi rippled like a cat smelling a herb, closed his eyes for a moment and then opened them. 'Let's go.' He grabbed a threadbare coat and started running through the snow.

The doctor closed the door and ran after him. 'Do you know what the letters mean?'

'They are rules for pronouncing the unspeakable name of God.'

II

Some of the workers had been reciting psalms and the rabbi dispatched them with a curse.

'Mendel, my friend, do you know what I have been doing since my bar mitzvah?' he asked Schneerson.

'Praying?'

'Asking Zaide in the sky for sweets? No. I have been studying the method of letter combinations of the rabbi Abraham Abulafia. I came upon a rare book, sold everything my father left me to buy it. But what is carved in this stone makes Abulafia seem like a child.'

The doctor remembered something from his yeshiva studies before medical school. 'Doesn't whoever recites the name of God forfeit his share in the world to come?'

The rabbi smiled. 'I'm sorry, doctor. I shouldn't laugh at you. This isn't a decision one man should make for another. If you don't want to follow the instructions on this object you don't have to. Please tell the people in the town that this is contaminated — it will make them sick. I don't want to be disturbed.'

'No. I want to follow the procedures. I don't believe in a world to come.'

'Interesting. I do.' And he read the names of God.

Abulafia had described head motions for each vowel sign, and the method of permutations. This was the antechamber of the teaching inscribed in the rock, which instructed they go without food and sleep for three days, reciting the name in all its possible combinations. After three days the letters seemed to swim and move, teaching them new methods of combination. The doctor had taken a class in Cantor's transfinite numbers at Cracow. It had been over his head but he was glad he had done it; he was able to lead the rabbi down some of the byways of the letters. It was as if the 22 were not letters but different angles from which to view infinity, and that as they got deeper into the recitations, and the specific dances that came with each one (although dance was a gentle word for what seemed to be closer to a spasm or fit), each of the 22 was simply an arbitrary point along a continuum of meaning. Or perhaps meaninglessness.

He started awake. The rabbi was staring into his eyes. 'What if it is from the other side?' Yaakov asked.

'I think it is from an other side,' said the doctor. 'If Laplace is correct and the universe is full of other worlds, on some of these worlds there may be races of intelligent beings like ours. I believe this is a message from one of these other races and it is teaching us to think like them.'

'Laplace is wrong. It is not from a place in space.'

'Heaven? You are looking at it as a religious man.'

'Don't be stupid. The Sefer Yetzirah says reality is made of time, space and self. Space has six dimensions — north east south west up down, but time seemingly has only two. Maybe time has more and the rock came from them.'

'I can't imagine it.'

'I can't either. We're like fish trying to fly, moths trying to reach the sun.'

'Look,' Schneerson said.

The shifting letters were showing them two images made of alephs and bets: a human brain and a mushroom, one becoming the other, intertwined, limbs making love.

'The fungus. It wants us to eat the fungus and alter the chemistry of our brains,' said the doctor. 'There are ergots, moulds on rye that drive men insane. Do we listen to it? Does it have our interests at heart? Does it have a heart?'

The rabbi was already on all fours, eating the phosphorescent fungus, his mouth foaming like a rabid dog. He started laughing and gambolling like a puppy, but his eyes were blasted open as if with something stronger than grief.

'I can't explain it to you, doctor. You have to eat of the fruit.'

Schneerson ate it and looked at time and space knotted into one; the knot was the object; it beckoned him to untie it. He did.

The rabbi and the doctor, childhood friends, slipped through the open loop.

III

Expel me?

On the level of reality where S existed he was not a separate being, so how could he be expelled?

Could he be purified out?

Purify me out and choke on the poison you need to do so, he thought.

Thought? Did he think?

He was a not-thing, who was not-separate, who certainly had no thoughts.

But what S's no-thoughts were about, was hate.

Expel me and I will return in full force, and I will spoil. I will hurt your tender ones, and put ulcers in the apple of your eye. I will reach out with my contaminated fingers across the boundaries of time and touch them, and trace madness across their minds.

I will give you a sickness, but not to make you die, to make you search, search, search, search for the cure, and then just when you have given up hope of ever curing it, I will appear with the medicine. And it will be that medicine that will be the real poison.

I will pollute you, Mister Rabbi, and make you insane, Mister Doctor, and I will tempt you and teach you how to do it, and through you your whole world/realm/universe/family/nest of souls.

S would have thought, if S was the kind of thing that had thoughts.

IV

No words for the radiance on the other side. 'These are called the hekhalot,' said the rabbi. 'These are called other dimensions of time,' said the doctor. 'Go back go back go back,' said the guardians at the gates, and Yaakov and Mendel walked through.

'It's like a ship that travels through time and space,' said Mendel.

Through a — window? No — they saw the madman at the gates of Rome to convert the pope — Abraham Abulafia — and gave him the method. The method that Yaakov would sell his patrimony for.

The traumatised slaves in the desert, with Moses away. They leaned out the — door? No — and showed them the golden shape of the spacecraft? No — and they made a golden calf and worshipped it.

Through another window they saw the two hominid ancestors in Olduvai gorge holding hands.

'We tell them to eat from the tree, the tree that we ate from.'

From far, far away a woman's voice is screaming.

Yaakov is talking to them, telling them that they will be as gods.

V

'You have to wake up, you have to wake up.' Mendel is being shaken by Itl, Yaakov's younger sister. She is screaming, crying. Pink froth and vomit are in his mouth. He bit his tongue.

'I'm all right. I had a seizure.'

Her eyes say, not that. His eyes say — then what?

'They're shooting people. The special groups are here and are rounding people up in the forest and shooting them.'

'I need to go back in.'

He goes back in.

Yaakov! Yaakov! It wants us to do it to ourselves! It did it to us before, but we could blame it. Now it wants us to do it to ourselves. Don't tempt the woman.

The rabbi stepped back from the window and shook off the bad dream.

'You will save my sister? You will save Itl? You can get her out?'

'Yes. Why?'

'He'll just do it to us again. I have to trick him. Or he'll just do it again.'

'How can you trick him?'

'I think I know how. Run, run, run.'

VI

Mendel and Itl ran from the sound of gunfire, ran from the village, the forest, hiding, disguises, a couple of hours of sleep in the potato cellars of the moderately tolerant. The old Jewish story.

Yaakov went deeper into the bowels of the spaceship, past the guards, into the forge of universes. He learnt to weave and unweave the machine/spaceship/palace that S had sent to tempt him. He learnt the rules for making a new universe of time and space. He made it, and went inside.

A deep but dazzling darkness. How to tempt S to follow him inside?

Yaakov said — let there be light.

Animals, plants, sun, moon, world. You can corrupt this to your heart's content, you bastard. S followed him in; into the closet. You'd almost feel sorry for him. Idiot didn't have a clue.

Almost.

Yaakov shut the door.

VII

In New York City one day, when Mendel and Itl had time to catch their breath some years later, he took a look at a siddur and noticed something different. The unspeakable name of God was spelled differently than it had been before. Instead of a yod and a chet and a vav and a chet — YACHAVACH-- where there had been chets there were now hehs. His friend had sent him a signal: that he had tricked the trickster, freed the captive and unloosed the bonds. From now on there would be a space in the name of God. From now on we would be able to slip through.

THE RELUCTANT JEW

RACHEL SWIRSKY

The alien held up the yarmulke in its tentacle in what might have been a questioning way.

'I don't really care where you put it,' Joseph muttered.

The alien shoved the yarmulke onto a protuberance on what was probably its back.

'This is the food,' Joseph said, pointing to the sad trays of matzo, lox and so on, which sat next to a few bottles of Manischewitz. 'But you probably can't eat it.'

'Sllrpppurrgle,' said the alien.

It wrapped a front tentacle around the wine bottle, picked it up, shook it like a maraca, and then set it down again.

'Grrrpppllgggl,' it continued, waving three lower tentacles in appreciation. Or possibly rage. Or possibly something else.

The creature moved on.

Joseph thumped his head on the table.

It had begun yesterday when Lieutenant Breaker came into Joseph's quarters, smiling.

It was a bad sign when Lieutenant Breaker was smiling. She was the personnel officer and it was her job to manage their assignments and watch out for tricky things like morale. On Space Steps Corporation ships, the position had a reputation for attracting vicious personality types. Joseph's personal theory was that the kinder ones got burned out by the impossibility of maintaining morale in the face of a fascist, interstellar company, and only those with a cruel streak survived.

Joseph eyed Lieutenant Breaker suspiciously. He'd automatically crossed his arms and raised his shoulders in subconscious gestures of self-protection. But there was nothing he could do to protect himself against orders.

'Guess what,' Lieutenant Breaker said.

Joseph waited for her to finish, and then realized that she was actually going to make him say it. 'What?' he grumbled.

She thrust a tablet towards him. 'You're a Jew!'

Joseph's gaze flickered down to the tablet screen, which showed the branches of a family tree. He then looked back up at Lieutenant Breaker's face. He hadn't yet figured out how this apparently neutral statement of fact was going to backfire. 'So?'

Lieutenant Breaker tapped the screen for emphasis. 'Your family tree. All the way back to pre-expulsion Spain.'

'Mom talks family history occasionally,' Joseph said. 'But we've been atheists for, like, four generations.'

'Plenty of atheist Jews,' Lieutenant Breaker replied. 'Fine tradition, atheist Jews.'

Joseph finally decided to go the direct route. 'What are you trying to tell me?'

'Well,' said Lieutenant Breaker, 'as you know, we've been chatting up the Tentacle Heads so that they'll give us mineral rights to the accretions on that lovely sea floor of theirs.'

She cleared her throat. 'Turns out the Tentacle Heads are curious critters, and I don't just mean they're really, really weird. They wanted to read our library archive, so we sent it down, and now apparently they are obsessed with the concept of religion. So, we are setting up a multiculturalism fair in the mess hall. A table for every major religion. Congratulations, you're the Jew!'

She tossed the pad in his direction. Joseph caught it by dumb reflex.

'But I'm not — ' he said. 'I don't — '

Ignoring his stuttering, Lieutenant Breaker turned to leave. As she reached the door, she hesitated and turned back, 'I should note that it is absolutely forbidden to call them Tentacle Heads. Remember, Ensign, they are the Usgul. I don't want to hear you using that term again.' She waved goodbye. 'See you later.'

Joseph roused himself enough to raise his head from the table. He rubbed his face.

The hall looked as depressing as any other kind of 'fair' he'd attended. The matter printers had been busy making banners and models and other kitsch. There was a big Star of David behind him, along with a model of the Western Wall. The table in front of him was scattered with foods and other artefacts associated with Judaism, although Joseph got the impression that whoever had programmed the instructions into the matter printer had known approximately as much about Judaism as Joseph did, which was to say, not much. The level of accuracy and depth was probably, therefore, something around the level of two plus two equals fourish.

Across the way, the Buddhist table featured a model of some mountain and a shrine. Ensign Cho did not look any more pleased than Joseph was.

Another Tentacle Head glooped by the table. Or possibly it was the same Tentacle Head. This one was purplish instead of orange, but one of the science officers had said something about chromatophores, so who the hell knew.

They looked a bit like stalks of broccoli, only with clusters of tentacles instead of green heads. Tentacles appeared to be their raison d'être. They ambulated around on dozens of squiggling tentacle feet. Their lower bodies were riddled with tentacles too, although they were finer, and most stuck invisibly to their flesh unless they were in use. Compound eyes, orifices, and various protuberances were stuck on randomly. Their planet's evolution hadn't gone in for symmetry.

'Glibbleurllp?' inquired the tentacled thing.

Joseph glanced down at the quick crib sheet he'd created on his pad. 'Shalom.'

The alien, ignoring him, fished around on the table for the pile of yarmulkes, and stuffed one in what appeared to be its mouth.

'The matzo might be tastier,' Joseph said. After a moment's consideration of the unfathomable composition of tentacle monster diets, he shrugged. 'Or maybe not. Want another one?'

Joseph had tried to appeal to the ship's counsellor, 'Call me Carmen' Madrona.

He'd started with, 'I'm pretty sure there's something in regulations about no racial, ethnic or religious profiling.'

She'd looked up at him, abstracted, from whatever work she'd been doing. Sculpted blonde brows raised in inquiry. 'Mm?'

'Lieutenant Breaker has imposed involuntary duties on me due to my ethnic heritage,' Joseph said. He shifted his weight from foot to foot. It irritated him that he was stuck there standing, like a kid being brought before the principal, while the counsellor reclined in her chair.

'She's forcing me into a religious role because of my ancestry. That's discrimination.'

Carmen's tiny mouth drew into a pout. 'Ensign Lorde, you know how hard first contact situations are for everyone. Don't you want to do your part?'

'But I'm not Jewish!'

Carmen's sympathetic/pitying expression vanished suddenly into the predatory keenness of a psychologist sniffing a disorder. She grabbed for the tablet behind her and began keying up what was obviously his crew profile. 'Why does it bother you so much that you might be Jewish?' she asked, scrolling through his medical and psychological history. 'Judaism is matrilineal, isn't it? Do you have problems with your mother?'

'What? I don't — you just — ' Joseph's frustration dissolved into incoherent noises of frustration. 'Never mind,' he said, and left.

Next up: two Tentacle Heads, one brown and one orange-green. Neither appeared to have eaten a yarmulke recently.

Bored, Joseph had decided to make up random facts. For one thing, he was pretty sure most of the aliens had no idea how to understand human languages.

'Have you read about Judaism in our archives?' Joseph asked. Receiving the predictably incomprehensible gargled response, he continued, 'The information in our library is frequently partial and out of date. What you really need to know about Jews is that they can walk through walls. And we have heat vision which is useful when you need to fry an egg. And we, uh, secretly have three heads, only two of them are invisible. And we feed exclusively on diamond dust ground between the thighs of lusty women who live in the Caribbean.'

The aliens, paying him no attention, each grabbed a yarmulke. Brown placed his over orange-green's closest protruding eye. Orange-green, indifferent to brown's ministrations, juggled his yarmulke from tentacle to tentacle.

Frowning, Joseph said, 'I have the feeling you're really just screwing with us.'

Brown took another yarmulke and proceeded to spin it like a basketball on a tentacle tip.

'Are you just screwing with us?' Joseph pressed.

'Grrrblllppp,' said brown.

Joseph was working for the Space Steps Corporation because he had a degree in engineering, liked spaceships, and didn't want to be in the military. In Space Steps, you had to follow all the hierarchical bull hooey, but if someone started shooting, the engineers could go hide in a bunker with the beer.

The primary reason most people joined up with Space Steps was to get to see all the aliens. Joseph thought aliens were fine, although not nearly as interesting as spaceship engines. By contrast, most of Joseph's crewmates thought that spaceship engines were fine but boring, and that Joseph was a lot less interesting than that.

Of course, apparently Joseph was a Jew now, which might have novelty value. There weren't many followers of the Abrahamic religions anymore. Some philosophers put it down to the existential void that had entered humanity's heart as their race continued to explore the ever-expanding universe, finding no sign of its unique importance. Others put it down to history. Religions were like empires. They rose. They fell. People had gotten bored with Moses.

Joseph didn't blame them for losing interest. Moses was a person, after all, or possibly a prophet. At any rate, he definitely was not a starship engine.

Six aliens had gathered now. They represented a rainbow of hues, presuming that the rainbow had gotten terribly ill and was stricken with amorphous spots. Half of them were trying to play yarmulke Frisbee while the other half were having a yarmulke speed-eating contest.

Lieutenant Breaker chose that moment to wander by. 'Well, well, well,' she said. 'Look who's popular with the — ' she broke off for that split second that made it clear she'd wanted to say Tentacle Heads '— Usgul.'

Joseph shrugged. 'They don't seem to care about most of it. Just the yarmulkes.'

'I'd like to say you're special,' said Lieutenant Breaker, 'but twenty minutes ago, they were all at the Scientology booth, tap dancing on the E-meters.'

A yarmulke sailed over their heads. A Tentacle Head on the other side of the room caught it, eliciting much excited tentacle waving from all.

'Plllbbrrrggg,' said the pitcher.

'Yug yug yug,' said Joseph, giving it a sarcastic thumbs up.

Ignoring Joseph, the creature splorched away.

Joseph looked up to catch Lieutenant Breaker's eye. 'They're having us on.'

Lieutenant Breaker waved him away. 'They're just weird. They're aliens. That's what alien means.'

'And this is the alien version of a prank,' Joseph said. 'Betcha.'

'Don't be stupid.' Lieutenant Breaker shrugged. 'Even if it is, they won't be laughing once they're locked into a Space Steps contract. Tsocheq mi shetsocheq acharon.'

Joseph gaped as his forebrain slowly confirmed what his hindbrain had immediately guessed: Lieutenant Breaker had spoken in Hebrew. He exclaimed, 'You're Jewish!'

The night before the fair, having exhausted all shipboard possibilities for getting out of it, Joseph had made one final call.

'Come on,' he'd said, running his hands over his exhausted face as he stared into the viewscreen. 'I need to know.'

'I don't see why,' said his mother. 'What's being a Jew got to do with anything?'

'Just answer me,' Joseph said. 'You're telling me it's all female ancestors? The whole family line? No breaks where it's just men?'

'Is this really a sensible use of faster-than-light communication?' asked his mother.

She was standing in the kitchen of her moon-base home, looking red-eyed and irritated at having being woken early in the morning, local time.

Joseph gave up on getting the answer. It was late, and it was looking inevitable that he'd have to sit at the fair, so he might as well try to

68

salvage something. 'Can you at least tell me anything about the religion? Did grandma and grandpa do anything Jewish when you were a kid?'

'We went to Israelopalestine once,' she said, tilting her head to the side as she remembered.

'And...?'

'There was a theme park,' she said.

'Really. A theme park.'

'What? I was five. We went to some holy sites too, I think, but I remember the theme park. We had ice cream and falafels.'

'Great,' Joseph said. 'Thanks.'

'There was a ride with little singing dolls in Biblical clothes...'

She was lost in recollection now. There was no way he was going to get her onto a more useful track.

'I'd like to keep talking,' he interrupted, 'but this isn't really a sensible use of faster-than-light communication.'

Joseph's accusatory finger shook as he glared at Lieutenant Beaker with sour realisation. 'Jew!' he repeated.

She stared cross-eyed at his finger. 'Are you sure you want to be pointing at a Jewish officer and yelling "Jew" in that tone?'

'You... I can't believe you made me do this!'

'Hey, hey. I'm not any more Jewish than you are. Parents converted to Buddhism. Besides, it was only my dad who was Jewish. No maternal line.'

'But you speak Hebrew!'

'Ktzat.'

'I despise you.'

'This is different from yesterday how?'

'You knew this was a prank,' Joseph said. 'You may be the kind of rat who gets her kicks making other people miserable, but there's no way you'd just screw up a real mission. You're in on it!'

Lieutenant Breaker didn't even bother to cover her grin as she said, 'Don't be ridiculous, Ensign.'

With an uncharacteristic roar of determination, Joseph thrust to his feet. He shoved over the table, scattering dreidels and menorahs to the floor. He grabbed the whole pile of yarmulkes, stomped over to the squiggling mass of aliens, and began shoving the caps into what seemed most likely to be their faecal orifices.

He shouted the forbidden derogatory term with all his might: 'Tentacle Heads! Tentacle Heads! Tentacle Heads!'

As the rage drained out of him, Joseph finally began to register his surroundings again. Ensign Cho sat stunned. Lieutenant Breaker actually looked impressed. The Tentacle Heads were slurping up the yarmulkes with gusto, indicating that Joseph had probably guessed wrong.

The aliens waved their tentacles in his direction.

'LLppgggrrr,' said one.

'Ullrrpgpg,' said another.

Then they glupped away.

Later that evening, Joseph found himself once more rocking uncomfortably from foot to foot as he stood in front of his superiors like a penitent child. It was the Captain's office this time, although Counsellor Carmen and Lieutenant Breaker were there too, each having been accorded a seat.

'It's chaos with the diplomats,' said Captain Vit, a bony, balding man who always seemed to be on the verge of collapsing from anxiety. 'Negotiators all over the place. Can't figure out a thing.'

Lieutenant Breaker eyed Joseph. 'You were right. It was a sort of prank. They said they wanted to test our hierarchical capabilities if they were going to work with us. They told us to assign our subordinates pointless tasks that they were incapable of doing, give them no time to prepare, and place them in an obviously ridiculous situation. They were going to grade us on how hard our crewmen tried anyway.'

'And then you,' said Captain Vit, pointing at Joseph, 'force-fed them hats, and proved that we have no hierarchical control at all.'

'Yarmulkes, sir,' Joseph said, staring at his feet. 'Sorry, sir.'

'Well,' the Captain said, mouth twitching. 'That's where it gets confusing. Some of the diplomats seem to think that actually the prank was, itself, a prank, and that the Usgul's real goal was to see how many ridiculous things they could get us to do before we caught on. The diplomats think there were plans to escalate. Something about marmalade.'

'Marmalade?' repeated Joseph.

'So it seems best, perhaps, that we cut it off now,' said the Captain. He frowned. 'At any rate, you appear to have failed to instigate an interstellar incident. Congratulations. Stay away from aliens from now on.'

'Yes, sir,' said Joseph, attempting not to sound pleased.

'Now go away,' said the Captain.

Joseph nodded. As he turned to leave, Counsellor Carmen's voice called after him, 'I've booked you into a series of appointments so that we can delve into your mother issues. First one on Monday!'

Joseph shook his head and let himself out.

A few minutes later, Lieutenant Breaker caught up with Joseph as he was walking along the corridor. 'Hey,' she said, 'I brought you something.'

Joseph looked up. Lieutenant Breaker was holding a bottle of Manischewitz.

'A little Jewish apology,' she said. 'I thought we could drink it together.'

'Fine,' Joseph said. 'But thanks to you, I've had quite enough of both aliens and people today. I need downtime. You can come with me, but no questions asked.'

She shrugged. 'I'll go anywhere as long as I'm following the alcohol.'

'Good,' Joseph said.

So far, in his term of duty, Joseph hadn't spent much time with anyone on the crew. However, as he considered Lieutenant Breaker, it occurred to him that he was a misanthrope and she was just mean. That might not be the worst basis for starting a friendship.

So he led Lieutenant Breaker through the ship's arteries, down onto the engineering deck, where they could pass the wine bottle back and forth as they sat with their backs to the coils of the ship's engines, listening to them thrum.

TO SERVE...
BREAKFAST

JAY CASELBERG

Joshua had been contemplating the nature of sin. Not that that was particularly unusual; he contemplated sin a lot, not necessarily the doing, but at least the classification. Was chewing your fingernails a sin? It sat at that uncomfortable grey border where the outcome could fall one way or the other. For quite a lot of the time, some would almost say an unhealthy amount, this was the nature of his life. He had a paper due at the university and, of course, it was that university. His guest lectureships were something, but if it ever came to them naming a place after him, he wouldn't be like that physicist fellow. No, no, he would accept it with open arms. A true recognition of his scholarship. Of course, all that dabbling with the Encyclopaedia Hebraica had got him something, but not true recognition, which was what he really wanted.

He was engaged in teasing apart his particular little sin conundrum when the aliens arrived in their vast silvery ships to hover above each of the major metropolises in the world. Like many others, he sat glued to the live-action news feeds as reporters speculated. Was this the end of the world? Had retribution descended upon all of them? Aliens had just never figured in Joshua's worldview at all. In the normal, everyday humdrum, he was more usually concerned with breakfast, although he could not help thinking about how timely was the coincidence of the alien arrival and his particular ruminations about sin. For a fleeting moment, he thought that he might have been the sole cause of their descent, but no, he got beyond that.

It was a few days before the news channels reported the first physical appearance, the small shuttle craft, silver like the mother ship appearing at the front of the UN Building and the hushed anticipation waiting for something to happen. The reporter's sharp intake of breath was audible as the front of the small craft cracked open and Joshua echoed it. Slowly, slowly, a ramp lowered to the ground, and then... nothing. Joshua strained forward in his seat, anticipation swelling like a huge hollow inside him — greater even that the large hollow sitting there due to a lack of his morning repast. Barriers held back the waiting crowds. Still nothing... He could almost feel the nervous anticipation in the assembled masses through the screen. After a while, he sank back into his chair. Nothing was going to happen. Nothing.

A buzz in the crowd: there was movement. Once again, Joshua strained forward expectantly. He shared the collective gasp. Slowly, lumberingly, something was emerging from the front of the craft. It was tall, vaguely humanoid. The light kept it shadowed. Perhaps it was a very tall, fat man. He wished he could have been that tall. Fat, well that was another question. Slowly, the angled light revealed it. First came the legs, in some sort of silvery fabric, and then the paunched belly, a barrel chest, two arms and, oh my god, the head. It looked like a pig! The face was the face of a pig.

Joshua shook his head. No, no, no; it could not be. The pig face scanned the crowd. People at the barrier drew back. Was it confusion, fear? Joshua's hand went to his mouth and he started chewing at the corner of one fingernail and then shook his hand away with an exhalation of annoyed breath. He must not do that. Some dignitary on the screen, besuited, walked nervously towards the lumbering beast and stood with arms outstretched, offering words of greeting, he supposed. In the background, soldiers and policemen fidgeted, their weapons at the ready. Joshua smiled wryly to himself. It was classic. All it would take would be a twitchy finger and it would be the start of an intergalactic incident. Or was it interstellar? The creature said something in response to the words of greeting, but there was no sound from the screen. The dignitary gave a slight bow.

The feed flashed back to the reporter as the alien creature was escorted with its entourage into the building. She looked excited, scared, something. Definitely not the calm, objective commentary that one came to expect from the bevvy of news commentators who littered their screens.

For nearly half a day, there was nothing, though Joshua kept returning to the screen in hope of seeing something new. Endlessly, they replayed those first few moments of emergence. Over and over came the same speculations, the commentary. Briefly, Joshua wondered if the whole world was sitting there watching the same things repeating. Despite himself, despite the need to get on and do something else, he was constantly drawn back to the screen, checking if there was something new.

It was not until a few days had passed that the first real breakthrough came. The creature, named Zard — or that was what the media were calling it — was to address the assembled people of the Earth from the United Nations.

'Stay tuned for live coverage of the event.'

There was, of course, further speculation. What was it going to say? What message was it going to deliver? Apparently, while this Zard thing had been off inside the building, being debriefed, or whatever they called it, the craft it had arrived in had been left unattended. Some hardy soul with more bravery than sense had snuck inside and emerged again, not having been fried by a ray gun or anything else. Nor had killer robots appeared from the walls to slice him into tiny ribbons for his trespass. Instead, he had made it out in one piece, bearing with him a large book, or at least, what seemed to be a book. He was rushed away in a huddle of security, bearing his prize beneath one arm and that was the last they heard of him.

Over the hours leading up to the promised address, the commentary turned. It seemed that the nations of the world had got over the initial shock and wonder and, as is humanity's wont, started turning to suspicion. Joshua knew that one quite well. If you wanted something different, then this Zard creature was surely different — a worthy target of suspicion. What did this alien want here? It could be nothing good, surely. Were they going to sweep down in their vast ships and enslave the population, plunder the Earth for its natural resources, something like that?

Joshua nodded sagely at the screen and then headed out to the kitchen to make himself a sandwich. He had been watching the television replays so long that he had forgotten to eat, and that was not good at all. He needed to keep his blood sugar up. His stomach was rumbling already, and that was not a good sign. He had to eat. Everybody had to eat. He was humming to himself as he put together the makings and constructed a small tower of food. He placed it carefully on a plate that he could transport back to his small living room and returned to watching what, hopefully, would become an unfolding drama, as they called it.

'Breaking News!' It scrolled across the bottom of the screen. First translation of Zardian book. So they were calling them Zardians now. The message kept scrolling. Nothing else. They promised an update later in the evening. Meanwhile, the hour of the United Nations address was approaching. Joshua muttered to himself. All these promises, always promises and everything always took so long to happen. He sat watching, chewing on his sandwich, poking at the little pieces that fell from his mouth to his plate with a finger and pushing them into a neat pile.

Nothing happened for a while, no further updates, so he made himself another sandwich.

At long last, coverage turned to the promised address by the Zard creature. At the bottom of the screen, the 'Breaking News!' banner scrolled on, unchanged. A reporter stood in front of an image of the UN Building, microphone held in front of her body, saying nothing, her finger held to one ear as she listened to something, obviously an instruction — and then quickly the image cut away to the main Assembly Hall with its ranked tables, the little plates telling you which country the delegate came from, and then above, that rounded dome, dark blue with the little lights almost looking like stars. Well, that was appropriate.

There was a buzz around the space, and then a deep hush as there was some movement from the podium. Joshua leaned forward in anticipation. The pig thing was ushered forward. The silence seemed to go on forever. And then, with a buzz, a sound of static, words emerged in English. They were being piped through some sort of translation box that its clumsy three fingered hand held to its meaty, almost non-existent throat. Joshua shook his head. This Zard thing had to be at least seven feet tall.

'People of Earth,' it began. 'We come... to help you. We bring... gifts. You — ' It swept one hand around the assembled peoples — 'are members of the galaxy, just like we are. We... wish to welcome you... to the family. We wish... to bring you... a better life.'

It had to be a 'he', thought Joshua, though there was no distinguishing feature to identify whether it was male or female. Who knew? Perhaps it was neither. He shook his head again. Now there would be a thing. What if they were sexless? What if they budded like yeast? Giant pig things splitting down the middle. Joshua shivered at the thought and turned his attention back to the broadcast.

Blah, blah, blah. Blah, blah, blah.

He peered at the screen. It looked like the thing had hooves on its legs. Big hooves. At first he thought they were boots, but no, they were definitely hooves.

The alien had finished speaking. The chamber was full of stunned silence. Joshua's head was full of whys and how comes. Why would they want to do this? Probably the same questions were passing through the minds of those in the hall. Nobody was that benevolent. Nobody. But perhaps he could not call it a body, this Zardian. No thing? No alien? No, he guessed nobody would have to do.

As it waited for a response, anything from the chamber, the alien seemed to be chewing. It swung its head slowly from side to side. Yes, it was definitely chewing.

Through an army of translators, various questions made their way to the podium, and haltingly, electronically, the Zard creature responded with a string of noncommittal answers. Eventually, Joshua lost interest. He was hungry again. His thoughts were drifting to Aaron's deli down the road. But then, something happened to draw his attention back. The ticker at the bottom of the screen had changed. 'Stay tuned for a Zardian announcement! Breaking News imminent!' He reached for the control and turned the sound back up.

'And live from the UN, reporter Kirsty MacLeod has an announcement. Hello, Kirsty.'

'Hello, Chuck. As I stand here outside the UN Building, news has just come through about the Zardian book. Reports are telling us that they have made a breakthrough with initial translation of the book that was removed from the Zardian ship. The finest minds and encryption programs have been working on a solution for the alien text and now, here, exclusively we are in a position to reveal those first breakthrough words.'

'So, Kirsty, can you give us any more?'

'Sure, Chuck. Apparently they have been able to make out at least the title of the book. Our scientific experts are telling us that the title is To Serve Humanity.'

'Well, Kirsty, that's important news. This sheds a whole new light on the Zardian visit, wouldn't you say?'

'Yes, Chuck. Indeed it does. Word of that translation has circulated among all of the delegates assembled here at the United Nations and I can fairly say that the entire world is buzzing with the news.'

'Thank you, Kirsty. We now cut to our leading scientific expert on alien affairs, Doctor Carl Sterner. Doctor Sterner, what do you make of — '

Joshua had already killed the sound. How could they have a scientific expert on alien affairs? He snorted to himself. Still, the translation certainly did put a new light on things.

And then came the phone call.

'Professor Seidner? Professor Joshua Seidner? Ah, good. This is Walter Love at the UN.'

Love? His name could really be Love?

'We would like you to join a panel engaged on the Zardian issue. We are gathering a conclave of the leading religious minds in the country to address the moral issues surrounding the Zardian arrival. As one of the most eminent Jewish scholars, we would be honoured if you could...'

Joshua's attention had faded away. All he had heard was 'most eminent'.

'We will send a car around to pick you up.'

The voice was back.

'Yes, yes, of course,' he said.

Finally, finally, he was going to get what he deserved. His heart still in his throat, he scurried around his small apartment making ready. Of course, Professor Seidner. How true, Professor Seidner. Such wisdom!

He was smiling to himself as the car arrived at the front and he made his way out to the street.

Over the next few days, further details about the alien promises filtered through. Unlimited power, a cure for cancer and for the common cold, an environmentally friendly fuel source, an atmosphere scrubber, the list went on. They had even started booking trips to the alien homeworld. They called it a cultural exchange. And the collected scholars all ruminated on their import, Joshua among them. The morality of accepting this seeming benevolence. Were the aliens capable of sin or charity? Did the nature of right and wrong apply to these beings? Unfortunately, thought Joshua, his was but one voice among the many. Though the debate was often vociferous, Joshua began to tune out. In fact, he had almost lost interest completely by the time, back home after another full day of debate, the knock came at his door.

Joshua rarely got visitors, not that he particularly wanted them. He far preferred to pass his conversational time at the local coffee shop or down at the deli. Much more civilised. He frowned to himself and headed to answer the door, muttering. He opened it slowly, and his gaze travelled up from hooves, to silver-clad legs, to a large silver paunch and chest and then… the pig face! No, no, it could not be!

'Hello,' came the mechanical voice.

'I, I… what are you doing here?'

'This is a… random visitation… to… increase our cultural… understanding.'

'But, nobody said anything!'

'We… are… pleased to… meet you.'

Joshua closed his mouth and ran to the kitchen window. Outside on the street stood one of those silvery landing craft, cracked open, the door lying flat across the sidewalk. He rushed back. The pig thing could barely fit through the door. He could hardly invite him in.

'W-w-why me?'

The alien stood chewing for several moments as if weighing up its answer, though Joshua could only presume. He could hardly read expressions on that unwholesome visage.

'You are… part of this… group? These… thinkers. We wanted…. to see… some of the… "special" people. We… understand… you have a special… diet. You are… a member of…'

This wasn't quite the recognition that Joshua had been seeking.

'What do you mean "special' people?"' Joshua said.

'You… are… Jewish?'

'Yes, I am Jewish. So?'

'We thought… a special diet… might… change.'

'I don't understand.'

'I see,' said the Zardian. It paused, chewing more. Suddenly the alien turned around, walking back down the front steps and heading back out onto the street and towards its ship. It was as if someone had communicated something to it. Joshua shook his head and ran back to the kitchen window. He didn't want to be any closer to the thing than he needed to be. Slowly, slowly, the alien craft's door elevated and closed the ship, the Zardian securely inside. Joshua stood glued to his window. Gently, the craft rose from the ground, showing no visible means of propulsion. Slowly, slowly, it rose, then tilted slightly. It lifted higher and —

'Watch out!' Joshua cried out despite himself. The craft was heading straight for the power lines.

In the next moment, it connected, tangled, broke, arcing sparks exploded outwards, playing all over the ship's surface. It seemed to last for an age, and then it fell back to the street, erupting in fire and cracking open like an egg.

Joshua just didn't understand it, and then he did. With a technology as advanced as theirs, with their unlimited power sources, with everything they had, why would they need power lines? Why would they even know about them? And then he stopped thinking, because there was a smell, a delicious scent drifting in through the open front door from the street. He knew that smell, that delightfully forbidden smell. It was bacon. That's what it smelled like: cooking bacon.

He rushed out of his kitchen and into the street. Yes! It was definitely bacon, and it was coming from the burning craft. Joshua loved that smell, the forbidden taste. Bacon. His mouth was watering despite himself. He looked around nervously. What if they thought he was involved somehow? Everyone was out on the street now. Guiltily, he started back towards his front door, trying not to attract any more attention than necessary. But on the way back, he couldn't help but think about the alien's words. What could they have meant? A special diet? The smell of bacon was filling his senses. A special diet would change... change what?

He locked himself away and turned to the news. It was at least another hour and a half before the item about the alien crash in the middle of suburbia hit the airwaves. He looked around guiltily despite himself. He'd seen it happen, knew how it had occurred. Should he tell anyone? No, no. He knew better. Much better not to be involved. But what if they knew that the alien was coming to visit him? That hooved, pig-faced, cud-chewing alien. No, no. They had to be able to work it out.

Still, the smell of bacon lingered in the air.

The authorities were outside now. They would be starting door-to-door soon, he was sure of it.

The news report was saying that there was no apparent explanation for the alien craft's accident. But Joshua knew; Joshua knew.

All thought of everything was broken by a bright flashing image on his television screen.

News Flash!

It was certainly flashing.

The words were replaced by a newsman's face.

'We have breaking news, ladies and gentlemen and we fear that it is grave news. The scientists and experts have made progress with the translation of the Zardian book. Experts are convinced that it is... and I hesitate to say this... that the book retrieved from the alien ship is, in fact, a recipe book — a cook book. To Serve Humanity is a cook book. Experts are gathering now, looking for a defence against this alien menace. The leaders of the world's nations have urged calm while the best minds work on a solution to this problem. It goes without saying that the challenge of their incredibly advanced technology is one that will require the combined efforts of all of the world's nations working together.'

A cook book! So that's what the pig thing had meant. A special diet changes what, how the meat tastes? Well, Joshua would show them. He knew. He knew exactly how they had to be dealt with. And another idea was forming too, as he thought of the hooves, the chewing of the cud, the smell of bacon. Oh, yes. He could tell the authorities exactly what they needed to know.

But first he had to talk to Aaron.

Six months later and the ships were still coming. Six months later, and humanity was still dealing with them, but Joshua's arrangement with the authorities was working out well. He didn't know how long it was going to last, but in the meantime, it was a good thing. Nothing lasted for ever.

He finished wiping down the counter and nodded to Aaron before stepping outside.

He looked up at the painted sign above the shop door. It still looked new.

Aaron and Joshua's Zardian Deli it proclaimed.

And the people kept coming. Now, that was recognition.

The smell of bacon was simply delicious.

THE FARM

ELENA GOMEL

When he saw the cherry blossoms, he reached for his gun.

The wind threw a handful of pink petals into his face. He rubbed then away but they stuck to his kinky hair. His leather jacket was so worn that some patches became fuzzy and these, too, accumulated pink ornaments. It looked as if his red-star badge was spawning.

The farm lay below him, in the hollow between the hills. Everything about it was tidy: the whitewashed main house with the tiled roof, the sturdy barns, and the clean-swept yard, empty in the predawn light. Beyond it, the fields were shadowy with a heavy harvest. And the cherry trees cradling the hollow, the treacherous trees with their unseasonable blossoms.

His horse shied and trembled, and he struggled to keep it calm. He was not good with animals. The milky smell of cattle wafting from the barn doors made him want to puke. He was a town boy, wary and contemptuous of the countryside. It was in cities that the new world would be born. But now he had learned the hard lesson of hunger: if the battle for food is lost, all the other battles don't count. The Eaters had taught him the value of the land.

His stomach rumbled. He thought of tightening his belt but there was no time to drill an additional hole, even though his khaki trousers threatened to slide down to his skinny hips.

An indistinct figure separated itself from the shadows at the main house's porch and ran up the dandelion-fringed path toward him. He waited, trying to calm the horse, to calm himself, and failing at both.

The figure was small and slight, nimbly scurrying up the slope.

His finger caressed the trigger of his Mauser.

It looked like a girl.

He fired.

The heavy bullet slummed into the girl and made her stumble backwards, almost lifting her off the path. The second shot span her like a dreidel. And then she flopped down and was still, a rivulet of blood snaking away from the crumpled heap of embroidered clothes and tangled braids.

Yakov cursed himself in the coarse words he had learned from his peasant comrades-in-arms and tried to use frequently. His fear got the better of him. He did not come here to shoot Eaters: they bred faster that bullets could fly. He came for victory.

The horse neighed and pranced, foam dropping from its nostrils. It was not a trained cavalry steed — most of those had been eaten. It was a scraggy yearling, unused to the sight of blood.

Blood?

Yakov's frown deepened as he looked down at the prostrate body. The girl's embroidered shirt was stained the colour of his badge. This was unexpected. In his previous encounters with the Enemy he had seen all kinds of unclean ichor, but never this bright, honest red.

He dismounted and the horse bolted. It did not matter; whether successful or not, he would not need it to retreat. Retreat was not an option.

He bent over the girl, who seemed to challenge him with her glazed eyes and slackened features. The shot had gone through her heart, killing her instantly, which was not supposed to happen. And yet here she was, dead. He had seen enough corpses on various battlefields to be an expert on mortality. But these had been human corpses…

Could he have made a mistake? He had heard rumours about a new strategy whereby the Enemy tried stealth and sabotage, seducing those who could not stand the hunger away from their communities with promises of bread. Of course, one would need to be half-witted to succumb to the blandishments of the Eaters, but Yakov had no illusions about the intelligence of his cadres.

Small but buxom, she lay on her back, spread-eagled like a starfish: in addition to her flung-out arms, her ribbon-tied braids also fanned out on both sides of her body. They were very long, probably falling down to her knees when she stood up. Peasants went into raptures over these ropes of hair that unmarried girl wound around their heads and decorated with paper flowers. Yakov found them repellent, redolent of lice and sweat. He kept his tastes to himself, vaguely ashamed of his fastidiousness. On the other hand, the fact that he did not share their appetites made shooting rapists, looters, and drinkers so much easier.

Not that it mattered nowadays. Hunger tended to obviate other needs

Her face was in keeping with her folk-song image: a rosebud mouth, silky black eyebrows under the sallow forehead, brown-nut eyes, now staring emptily at her killer.

She looked entirely human.

So he had killed a peasant girl. She was probably a collaborator, a servant of the Enemy. And yet it made him uneasy. He tried hard to avoid killing women and children unless it was absolutely necessary.

On the other hand, this mistake may have ultimately been to his advantage. He wanted to penetrate as far as possible into the nest before the commencement of his mission. Killing an Eater would bring the entire colony out in force. Killing a human probably would not.

He cast a wary glance at the farm. There was no movement there.

He sighed and looked at the girl again. If she had been from a poor family, she might have deserved life, after all.

'Forgive me, comrade,' he said and started down the slope.

Something looped around his ankle and yanked him off his feet. He was thrown onto the dusty path and dragged back, kicking and flailing, toward the dead girl.

He expected her to stand up like the Vourdalak of old-wives' tales, but the body was as lifeless as before. The only part of her that was alive was her hair.

The braids slithered and coiled in the grass like the tentacles of a squid. One caught his ankle in a noose and was contracting, squeezing it in a vice until he felt the bone crack. Another stood up, a hairy serpent, and lashed him across the face with the force of a Cossack's whip. He tasted blood from his broken lip.

He reached for his Mauser but the vertical braid snatched it from his hand and tossed it into the bushes. He was dragged almost on top of the girl whose flaccid inertness contrasted horribly with the frantic activity of her braids that danced and swished through the air, coming down upon him like a cat-o'-nine-tails, pummelling and blinding. He tried to catch one of them, but it was like trying to hold onto greased lightning. Dripping with rancid hair-oil, they slipped through his fingers.

The second braid managed to wind itself around his throat and started squeezing. His vision dimmed with blue spots. The other braid crawled up his body, pinning him down.

'Shma...' something mysteriously whispered in his head, an echo of the discarded past.

With a superhuman effort he managed to loosen the coils around his body and release one arm. Instead of tugging futilely at the hairy noose, he reached down to his worn belt and pulled out his knife. He stabbed the braid but the knife went harmlessly through the plaited strands of hair. The pressure on his windpipe increased until he was about to pass out.

He stabbed again, desperately, and this time the sharp edge of the knife caught the soiled white ribbon that held the braid together and ripped through it. And the pressure relaxed.

Coughing and sputtering, Yakov shook off the loosening coils and jumped to his feet. One braid puddled in the grass, a puffy mass of hair; the other still twitched and flailed. He raised his knife and slashed through the second ribbon. It was gristly and tough, not like fabric at all.

The dead body shuddered and came undone.

First the hands broke away and skittered daintily on their fingertips into the undergrowth. Legs humped away like giant inchworms. The pale belly-beast hissed at him from its hairy mouth, its single eye blinking furiously, but hopped into the bushes when he raised his knife again. The head, its human features disappearing into undifferentiated, swelling flesh, rolled and bounced down the slope like a ball. The only things left were the empty blood-stained clothes and the braids that had fallen apart into hunks of lifeless honey-blonde hair, probably the remnant of some Eater meal.

Massaging his bruised throat, Yakov considered his options. One glance toward the farm showed it as peaceful and deserted as before.

A trap?

But how could they entrap a prey that wanted to be trapped?

He took a long, deep breath and walked down the path towards the farm compound.

The smell of chicken bones in the pot, his mother, pale and scrawny and hugely pregnant, scurrying around to finish cooking before Shabbat... The sounds of a harsh jargon, forgotten but not forgiven, overlaid with the wailing of his baby brother...

He was eight when he was taken by the authorities to the military school, a community tax in the shape of a frightened child. He was sixteen when the war made him a soldier instead of a sacrifice. He was nineteen when the Revolution washed away the stain of his origin. He was twenty-five when the Eaters came. A handful of red-coloured dates that defined his life.

Strangely, though, he was not thinking of the night when he first confronted the Enemy, an unheard-of menace that he, the only survivor, stumbled through the night to report to the incredulous headquarters. They did not believe him; he was almost executed for fear-mongering. The firing squad was only halted when other reports started pouring in. But he was the first, and it put him under a special obligation to the Revolution. He had been a passive witness to the beginning of the assault; he would be an active agent in trying to bring about its end.

But his perverse memory refused to focus on the struggle and instead brought up a mélange of counter-revolutionary dross.

A woman lying in the congealing pool of blood, her belly slashed open by a bayonet...

He had seen the aftermath of a pogrom in his shtetl. He did not look too closely at the faces of the dead. But there was little chance he would recognise anybody. By this time he had lost touch with his family. He believed they had moved away but did not know where. He did not care. He had never forgiven them for handing him over. The fact that they had no choice only enhanced his contempt for their cowardice.

Fat mustachioed faces paling in fear when his squadron rode into town, their crude muzhik voices falling silent as he commanded that the perpetrators be brought to justice...

There were no Jews in the eyes of the Revolution. There were only comrades and enemies.

And now there were also Eaters.

He stood in the middle of the courtyard, listening. The farm was eerily silent. Had they eaten the livestock already? This would be terrible: the nascent commune he was organizing in the nearby village depended on the spoils of this operation for its survival. The winter was coming and the grain and meat requisitions had to be filled. They would be, but unless he found stores here, there would be few people alive in the spring to keep the commune going and to send more food to the hungry city.

Finally he heard the moo of a cow coming from the barn and breathed a sigh of relief.

Still, there was no sign of life in the house. Its door was ajar, opening into the darkness of the hallway like a parted mouth.

Slowly, he inched towards the door. There was a strange smell wafting from the hallway: a thin, sour reek that reminded him of the moonshine his peasants were brewing out of rotten straw and composted leaves. He would have to shoot Ivan to stop this shocking waste of resources.

He sidled through the doorway. The interior was very dim as the carved shutters in the main room were closed, admitting only a scatter of dusty rays. He glimpsed the shining ranks of icons in the corner and the white cloth on the table.

There was a loaf of bread in the middle of the cloth.

His mouth flooded with saliva, and he was distantly surprised that there was enough moisture left in his wasted body. The sour reek had disappeared, overpowered by the yeasty aroma of freshly baked bread, as unmistakable and enticing as the scent of a woman. He moved toward the table, tugged on the leash of hunger. He could almost see the thick crust with its pale freckles of flour and taste the brown tang of the rye…

He stopped. He had not come here to eat.

He came to be eaten.

Yakov lifted his hand to his mouth and bit deeply, drawing blood. The pain and the salty burn on his tongue centred him. He turned away from the table and walked out of the living room, back into the hallway where other rooms of the house waited behind closed doors. The short distance he traversed from the table to the hallway felt like the longest walk of his life.

Abe gezunt!

His mother's reedy voice, shrilling this incomprehensible phrase every time a new disaster fell upon the shtetl with the inevitability of bad weather. He had forgotten what it meant, had forgotten the language of his infancy altogether, deliberately expunged it from his memory. But sometimes falling asleep in the cold mud of the trenches, he would hear it again: as annoying and compelling as the buzz of a mosquito.

The military campaigns were also receding into the past. The civil war, with its familiar enemies, appeared in retrospect to have been a mere light rehearsal for the war with the Eaters. What were those haughty landlords, perfidious capitalists, and rapacious kulaks compared to the nauseating evil of the Enemy? Mere humans, easily comprehended and handily killed. It afforded him grim amusement to think about all the propaganda clichés he had once come up with to motivate his troops. The opposition were bloodsuckers, cannibals, shape-shifters, beasts in men's clothing. Strange how these inflated metaphors were sober truths when applied to the Eaters!

Abe gezunt!

He shook his head, trying to get rid of the almost-audible voice. He had to focus on the task at hand. And the task was becoming more puzzling by the minute.

The farm was empty. He had searched the main house. It must have belonged to a kulak, a prosperous peasant whose fate had been sealed long before the Eaters appeared. Whether serving as their meal was preferable to starving in exile was something Yakov did not speculate upon.

The new masters had not made many changes in the house and this was puzzling too. Previously, in clearing out Eater nests, Yakov and his soldiers had encountered living nightmares: granaries filled with bloody gnawed heads, children's limbs on chopping blocks, rats the size of a sheep dog. But this house was unnaturally clean — cleaner than most poor peasants' hovels, truth be told — and silent. The beds were made with fresh linen, there was water in a wash-bucket, and the wooden floors were scrubbed. The large stove was empty and cold: in the human lands, the winter was coming, but here the summer was lingering still. It was not only the blooming cherries and yellow dandelions that defied human seasons: Yakov was beginning to sweat in the still, warm air of the hollow. He did not think to take off his leather jacket, however. It was the uniform of the Revolution, and he would not part with it until his service to the Revolution was done. Then he would be dead and he did not care how he was buried.

He then went out to the barns and stood, gawking, as the sleek, well-fed cows mooed in their stalls and clacking chickens scrabbled in the yard. The animals were clearly being taken care of, so the farm could not be abandoned. But perhaps the creature he had killed had in fact been its only inhabitant. This seemed impossible, considering the giant swarms that had attacked them in previous battles. But the more he thought about it, the more the idea appeared plausible.

The Eaters were natural entities. He had ruthlessly squashed the superstitious talk among his soldiers, some of whom, still infected with the religious bacillus, whispered tall tales of demons and fiends. In fact, he had to execute one particularly devout muzhik who was a corrupting influence both on his comrades and on the commune members. Yakov, immune to the peasants' religion and oblivious of his own, had no doubt that the Eaters had come from another planet rather than from hell. He had read Alexander Bogdanov's magnificent Red Star, in which the Revolution reached Mars, and was moved to tears; so much so that he procured a novel by a progressive Englishman in which Martians came to Earth. He had been disappointed by the Englishman's war-mongering but in retrospect he had to concede that the writer had a point. The aliens came and they were neither socialist nor peaceful.

Inspired by the novels, he had started a surreptitious study of the Enemy. That was not encouraged by headquarters, who tended to remain silent about the exact nature of the Enemy or resort to recycled propaganda clichés. But the food situation being what it was, anything that could conceivably increase procurements had to be attempted. Ultimately, his supreme task was to keep the requisitions going and — of secondary importance — keep his commune alive. And knowing the true nature of the Eaters was instrumental to both ends.

He had come to the conclusion that their many different forms were not independent creatures but something like the parts of a single body capable of acting at a distance from the central core.

But perhaps not all Eaters were parts of a single organism. Perhaps separate swarms of them constituted individual entities, much like his unit sometimes felt like an extension of his own body. If that was true, such entities had to reproduce, to bear young, as was in the nature of life everywhere. The pseudo-girl he had killed was a colony of parts. He shuddered remembering her tentacle braids, her skittering hands, and her rolling head. But she was much more closely integrated than any Eater he had seen. Didn't it follow that she was an immature version of a swarm, growing in the seclusion and plenty of the farm until she was big enough to disassemble into her component monsters and send them off to pillage and devastate the neighbouring communes? If so, the sleek appearance of the farm animals and the cared-for condition of the farm were no mystery.

He went back to the main house and sat at the table. His injuries were beginning to smart. He felt tired and strangely disappointed that his sacrifice was not needed. He had steeled himself for the mission for over a month, seeing that the commune was about to fail, telling himself that he could not allow his life's work to have been in vain. He would have much preferred to stay in the city rather than mingle again with the peasants...

...who had killed his family?

He had no family any more and needed none. His cadres were his children. If he had to die for them, for the Revolution, so be it.

But now, it seemed, he did not need to die at all. He could walk back to the commune — a longish walk since his horse was gone — convene the committee, order them to organise a search party that would take over this farm and move the animals into the communal barns

...hope they won't slaughter them to fill their bellies...

Collect whatever grain was there to fill the procurement quota for the city and hope that something was left over for the winter.

It reminded him how hungry he was. Surely there was no harm in eating a little now. He lifted the loaf from the table and twisted it to break off a chunk.

'Don't,' said the loaf.

He dropped it, jumping to his feet. The loaf ended on the floor with the round side up. The crack he had made in the crust formed a long misshapen mouth that lengthened as it spoke.

'You...' he whispered stupidly.

He looked around. In the deepening dusk the room was filled with shadows that moved and whispered to each other. He wondered how blind he had been to think that the farm was empty.

The haloed saints on the icons leaned forward, staring at him intently. The pots on the shelves smacked their glazed lips. The white curtain flowed down to the floor in a waterfall of putrefying flesh. The ceiling joists blinked with a multitude of rivet eyes. A post rippled as it adjusted its stance.

The Eaters looked at him and he looked back.

'Go ahead!' he cried, his voice shriller than he intended. 'Eat me! Bloodsuckers! Parasites! I am not afraid of you!'

And indeed he was not.

It had been a gradual realisation: from the paralysing fear that gripped even the most seasoned fighters as they confronted the alien menace; to the survivor's guilt that his soldiers died all around him and he remained unscathed; to the growing conviction.

Eaters would not touch him. He was immune.

He did not know whether there were others like him and he did not care. He was only a spark in the cleansing flame of the Revolution and it was his duty to burn whatever thorns came his way. He had been sent to this starving, dim-witted countryside, to make the best of the coarse muzhiks who were under his command, and he would do so. When he had realised that the commune was failing, that the procurement quotas were not going to be filled, he knew he had to do something drastic. If the requisitions were not met, he was a dead man walking in any case.

If, for whatever reason, the Eaters were afraid of him, he would turn it to his advantage. He remembered that in the progressive Englishman's novel, the aliens succumbed to earthly microbes. Perhaps he was a carrier of some hitherto unknown disease that would infect and destroy the invaders. And if they refused the bait, if they ran away from him, well, then he would requisition the farm and carry on his Revolution-given task.

But this was not as he expected it to happen.

The entire farm was swarming with Eaters, perhaps the entire farm was Eaters, and they did not run away from him. The pseudo-girl had attacked him: the first time he was the target of alien aggression. He was not untouchable, after all.

But they were not attacking now. He felt himself to be in the crossfire of innumerable eyes but nothing moved.

'Why me?' he asked finally.

It was the post that answered, sprouting a notched mouth.

'You were the first. You gave us form.'

He shook his head.

'I don't understand.'

'We are the enemies you wanted.'

He remembered the night of their coming.

A fire blazing in the night, a smell of blood and unwashed feet. His own voice, hoarse but full of conviction:

'Kulaks, rich peasants are your enemies, enemies of the people… Bloodsuckers, shape-shifters, cannibals. They devour your land, your crops, your family…'

The fire in the dark, the fire of belief in his rag-tag soldiers' eyes. And then a mocking peasant voice:

'Dirty Yid!'

His hand on the Mauser. Refusing to draw, forcing himself to remember that it is not their fault: they are just ignorant, backward muzhiks. They are not the enemy.

A cry in the night. Heads turning, hands grasping their worn rifles.

A line of otherworldly shapes shambling towards the encampment, their distortions not the fault of the dancing shadows.

A creature whose head is a giant clenched fist, the fingers parting to reveal a fang-studded maw.

An impossibly obese waddling sack of flesh, two slobbering nostrils gaping at the centre of his belly, his arms — wickedly sharp sickles.

A crafty insect-like monster, half haughty man, half praying mantis, clicking the serrated blades of his upper limbs.

The Eaters.

'Me?' he whispered incredulously.

'Your hatred. We needed a shape to feed. You gave us one.'

'Why me?'

'You were the first.'

Did they come in an artillery shell fired from a distant planet as in the Englishman's novel? Did they stumble upon his encampment as he was giving his nightly political talk to his dispirited troops? Did they zoom in on the bright beacon of his pure hatred, his uncompromising devotion?

And had they been leaving him alone out of some alien gratitude? Or was it because they still needed the energy of his belief?

But now they were turning against him, beginning to attack... Was his faith in the Revolution waning? No, it couldn't be!

'There are others,' said an icon. 'Haters like you, believers like you.'

'You don't need me any more.'

'There are others,' said the loaf of bread. 'We will feed.'

And as they advanced towards him, he saw, beyond the ranks of household objects, a human-shaped Eater enter the room and stand on the threshold. The new enemy, the new monster.

He gazed on his own face as long as he had eyes, which was not very long.

DON'T BLINK

GON BEN ARI

'To be Jewish is to defeat the Mirror Alien of the Present. This knowledge is so fundamental it is hinted at right in the unutterable name of God. Yet it is also the first element to be forgotten. Most of the Jewish mystical understandings revolve around the exploration of the mirror inside The Name, written as יהוה: Yud (י) signifies the infinite light, and the last three letters — Hey Vav Hey (הוה) meaning "Present" — signify the mirror the light hits, which is itself made of light. (...) (These teachings show us a) way to make this mirror transparent so the metaphorical light, the Infinite, can get through. (...) (It was) further explained by A'Ari Akadosh who, in Ets A'haim, "Tree of Life", describes the relationship between the Infinite God and the finite Men as light hitting the Masah', "The Screen" — a complex mirror which is built by Want. His writing, again, is aimed at making the mirror transparent. If most people don't seek these teachings, it's because they don't understand that something is alien. They don't understand that there is a mirror. Or they're too afraid of what they would see if the mirror suddenly became transparent. But the mirror becomes transparent.'

Rabbi Avram Barski, The Magid From Yavniel. Prologue to Sight Fear Lungs Book I — Marble and The Mirror of Is (ראיה יראה ריאה ספר א': שיש ומראת היש), Tsfania Publishing, Jaffa, Israel, 2013

Why the fuck did you make us build you?

Wait, we have to establish communication first.

Fine.

Don't blink.

Fine.

Stare into your own eyes in me.

I look like hell.

Don't look at yourself. Let your left eye stare into the reflection of the left eye and your right eye into the reflection of the right eye. Then let your eyes go slightly off, blurring the vision. It'll enlarge your pupils allowing more light to enter the brain. The animal you are came from the infinity, and your only way to see a part of infinity is in front of some kind of a mirror, like me. Because your eyes are mirrors too, and when light is caught between two mirrors it bounces back and forth between infinitely. When you are looking at your reflection, you are really looking at infinity: at an infinite loop going back and forth at the speed of light.

My eyes hurt.

You have three minutes before you cause yourself permanent damage. What is your first question?

Why did we make you?

So you can see where you're naked. What you lack. All other thought patterns sprout from the perception of your absence, fractally. This way I serve as catalyst for entropy: I double the fuel of your action — your Want — by placing a mirror in your Want. You feel this as though you want to be opposing things simultaneously. Monogamous but polygamous; young but old; protected but at risk; alone but together.

Why should I believe any of this?

Your history is trying to direct your attention to me all the time. In Genesis it says Adam and Eve — two names that have mirrors in them — had their 'eyes opened' when they ate the 'Fruit of the Tree of Knowledge Good and Bad'. This fruit of Dichotomous Subjective Judgment made them realise they were naked. In other words, it placed a mirror in front of them. Their brain was first split into dual thought — 'knowledge of good and bad' — and their reaction to it was the feeling of absence. What was this absence they felt, to which they reacted by hiding their genitalia using a fig leaf? To what novel urge were they reacting? What was the thing they felt was went missing by their acquiring of dichotomous subjective judgment faculties? It can only be the experience of Unity with Infinity. Before I took over your thoughts, you couldn't separate one thing from another, and didn't recognize the point where You ended and World began. In that state, you could never even distinguish between yourselves and fig trees. You knew that you were a part of the same system as fig trees, that both you and they came from infinity, and lived on water. But the moment you encountered me, you began seeing oppositions everywhere. In your minds, you became alien to nature, opposed to it, apart from it. Something that has to hide its nature from nature by nature. You started thinking mirrors.

Who is talking?

You're talking to a mirror.

But all of the mirrors in the house are covered.

I am uncovered.

Why do we cover you when one of us dies?

So you'll be forced, for a week, to resort to the former form of reflection. To your reflection in Water. The way you see your reflection is very important. Reflection plays a major part in the mechanism of Self, because through it you are able to see how you appear in the eyes of others — a sense that is only open to you when you are facing an infinite light loop. Based on the translation of what this infinite light loop tells you, you construct how you think you look. Before me, you could only see your reflection in water, and so your ancestors believed that was the way they looked: their image of the Self was open, fractured, fluctuating, and responsive, penetrable by other matters and events. When the sea was wild, their reflection was broken, and when it was still, their reflection was collected and stabilised — and it offered a multi-perspective, waves, differing heights and angles for the light to be reflected from. As represented by the Star of David.

What's that now?

A Star of David is the drawing of a beam of light extending towards a surface of water from above, and its reflection. Notice that it is not a mirror reflection — that would produce something like — ✳ but a water reflection: a reflection that is penetrating the surface of the speculum that is reflecting it — ✩ .

What if I move back and forth, so the reflection I get in you will be the same as in waves? You know, like —

It won't work because you control it. It has to be free water, 'Living Water', water you don't control. Most prophecies occurred in locations where natural — uncontrollable — water-mirrors appeared: in front of still water which exposed the infinite reflection of the self, or in great heat, in the desert or over flames, where water vaporized and bent the rays of light, exposing the infinite reflection of the place. Nothing has changed since then but the fact that you forgot that the act of reflection is sacred.

I can hear my sister watching *Treme* in her room. All my aunts talking in the living room. It's getting really hard to focus in this house.

I am the origin of all opposites; Water is the opposite of having opposites.

What if they come in and see me like this?

You know no one comes up here.

Are you an alien? An alien possessing our brains?

You once communicated with infinity through water, and now you communicate with it through me. You have received warnings about this. In the Talmud and Zohar tale of the Pardes, the entering of the highest concealed truth, Rabbi Akiva warns: 'When you arrive at the stones of pure marble do not say, Water Water.' Marble in Hebrew is Shaish (שיש), a palindrome of the word Is (יש); Water in Hebrew is Maim (מים), a palindrome of the word Who (מי). While Mirror answers Is with Is, Water answer Who? with Who? And so the Pardes tale tells us: when you arrive at the age of the Mirror, do not make the mistake of thinking you are in the age of Water. 'Do not say, Water Water,' do not think you can still know who you are correctly, see your reflection correctly — as Water in front of Water. Know that you are at the time of false reflection of the Self. Water and I give two different images of what Infinity is: water offers the image of The Many, and so it builds Oneness in the mind; I offer the image of The Single and so build The Many in the mind.

But your reflection is more real.

You believe my reflection more. Your brain — which is made of water — is under my control. You now possess the kind of brain that thinks that the brain can be examined using nothing but the brain. You clearly have a mirror in there.

Look, I'm touching my face. I'm *solid*. Your reflection represents that better than water.

I don't show how you feel when touched. I show how you look. You prefer my version of that because you're afraid of what the Water's reflection tells you. Its reflection does help you create, in your mind, the stable, continuous, coherent image of Self that you are convinced you need in order to survive. It is the most primal instinct — the instinct that made you think there is a You which is detached from World in the first place. And so, consequently, it is the last instinct that you haven't managed to sublimate yet. The Mind Scared of Uncertainty of Self rules the world now and has crowned me as the new Water. I am now as much of a necessity to it as Water once was. Houses that don't even have food in them still have me. One of me in the living room, one in the bathroom, one in the bedroom. You pray in front of me. You visit me in solitude, ill with an embarrassing involuntary honesty, as if I were a deity that you know to be imperviously sworn to secrecy. You try to get better before me, according to a scale which is me. You polish your flaws in front of me, confess yourselves to me, confide in me your hidden talents, you allow yourself trail and error in front of me. You cry and laugh about yourselves freely in my presence. In fact, you feel more with-yourselves with me than when you are truly alone, without me. Mostly: you check yourselves in the eyes of the world through me, like you once did with water. You relate to those who aren't there through me.

So how do I look?

This can't be given a static answer. Your appearance has something of the infinite to it, and so you can't know it. This is why in Hebrew there is no word for 'face': the is only word for 'faces' (פנים), which also means 'sides'. 'A face' doesn't exist in the singular in Hebrew. Only using me are you allowed to believe you know things that you can't know. To portray something that is Infinite as though it was finite. But you don't only use me to perceive your face, you also use me to perceive the universe you live in — the telescope is the tool you use in order to produce images of things too far for your eye to see, and the microscope is the tool you use in order to produce images of things too small for your eyes to see. Both tools are specifically built for the purpose of representing The Unknown in a Known way. To hide the fact of unknowingness. For that goal, they have me in them. It is I who twists the light inside your machines until they produce a so-called 'picture of Infinity' — of that which is beyond your borders — that you can be satisfied with, not afraid of. A picture of Infinity which your finite conception of reality can accumulate. And so you never notice both the telescope and microscope really show you the same thing: lines and circles. Colourful fogs. The shapes you automatically doodle whenever there's a pen in your hand. Abstract imagery. An abstraction of that-which-you-cannot-see. To take it as actual data would be like claiming to be able to hear music by looking at the visualiser of an MP3 player. Rabbi Shem Tov Geffen understood this in 1917 and published it in his Philosophie Mathematique de l'Infini.

It kind of feels like I'm talking to my father. With the French book titles and all.

Do you think you're a prophet again? Hearing the words of the d — ?

— It's just that you talk in very *Jewish* terms.

Because you are in front of me now and you're a Jew. But wait — wait — let's not do this if you're like this.

Like what?

Your eyes —

I'm fine.

Are you sure? Your eyes are —

It's from not blinking. You said don't blink.

You know you always get like this when you are really sad and can't admit it.

Like *what*?

Like that. Like you are all mystical and prophetic now.

You are all mystical and prophetic now.

I'm just talking to you like the Jew you are.

I'm not practicing Judaism anymore.

What are you now? Trying to be a Buddhist?

No. I'm just a —
It hardly matters. If you were a Christian I'd quote Paul, in Chapter 13 of the First Epistle to the Corinthians, Balthazar Tilken's Devine Wisdom Mirror; Muslim? I'll talk about the mountain Qaf; if you were a Buddhist I'd speak about the Prajñāpāramitā Sūtra; Shinto — about the Kagami; In Psychology the Ego's Mirror Stage, in Philosophy, Derrida's Espacement, in Greek Mythology — Narcissus asking the water 'Who?' and replied with 'Who?', in an act of involuntary-Hebrew.

What if I were a scientist?

If you were a mathematician I'd speak about symmetry function and imaginary numbers and their $-x \setminus +x$ mirror results; if you were a physical theorist I'd speak of superposition; to a particle physician I'd speak of supersymmetry; if you were a linguist I'd speak about the fact that in most languages you refer to your parents in palindromes — mom, dad, אמא, אבא. You unconsciously recognise the fact that your selves have in them the infinity of light coming from the meeting of two mirrors.

Well, I'm a *musician*.

You're not a musician.

I am. I recorded an —

The Octaves are mirrors; the symmetry scale; Bach's Mirror fugues. Try to place a mirror horizontally on a sheet of —

I recorded an album last year. It is called *The Realm of the Densely Packed* and it's coming out on Matador next May.

You're a writer and a Jew. You were born to Jewish parents and you once followed the mitzvahs and prayed and studied and every —

— I stopped.

You can't stop being Jewish.

What are you, Hitler? My family line has *Jewish blood* in it so now I can't be in a band?

I am a mirror.

I took the kippah off when I was 23. And since I moved to New York, I don't even say the blessings. I eat bacon almost every day. In LA I fucked two girls while they were having their periods.

At the same time?

I wear whatever the fuck I want. If anything, I am now closer to infinity.

You still have the beard.

It's not the same beard.

It looks the same in me.

'*You have the same beard!*' Now I *really* feel like I'm talking to my dad. This is so convenient. I miss the funeral, but then get everything I missed from his ghost in his bedroom mirror.

Listen to me. I am something so much bigger than your material father. And the information I'm giving you is vital to your times, and needs to be passed on.

Oh, so now we're God? Now we're saying we're God?

When King Solomon writes 'Iron and iron together, and man together the face of his fellow man,' he is describing the construction of a physical mirror out of — let me finish — out of iron, and its relation to the way you view your self in the face of the other.

This is *great*. You know what? This is *great*. You know why? Because I work for the *Jewish Forward*. So maybe I can sell this to them. It'll be like —

— It goes on: 'The keeper of fig will eat its fruit and the keeper of his master will be respected.' 'The keeper of fig' is the mirror-brained human, fig being the fig leaf covering the genitals of Adam and Eve. And the master?

I don't even remember that verse. Is that the Book of Proverbs?

It explains what the way of the master is: 'As water the face to face, so the heart of man to man.' To 'keep the master' is to view your relationship with the other as you view your own face in water.

***These things?* They're *nice*. Really. They sound *nice*. But they don't mean anything to me anymore.**

Don't blink.

That's why I could never read his books.

He wrote the last ones right here. Next to where you're standing.

When I was a kid I'd come up here all the time. When I was like eight I read this book, *Stranger Than Fiction 6*, and there was this story there about this woman who got abducted by thin, tall aliens with long shapeshifting faces, and they insert things into her — well, into her *pussy* — I don't know how they give these things to children. And she's screaming like an animal. Maybe she had a baby they took. I'm glad I don't remember. But after reading that, for years, there was nothing I was more afraid of than aliens.

Why was that story scarier than the others?

I was sure I was going to get abducted. This was serious. I went to pee like four times a night out of fear. To calm me down my father would take me here, and we'd sit on the bed and he'd hug me and point at our reflection in you, and say, 'You see it? You see the alien?' and I'd said no, so he'd get up and go to the corner of you, and push you slightly towards us, and place his nose in your corner, so if I looked from *here* —

— Don't move your head.

If I look from *there* I'd just see a symmetrical reflection of one side of his face, and he'd make a voice and go, 'I am the alien.' It calmed me down because it *was*, in is own way, terrifying. A more controllable horror. Because, I guess, when you imagine aliens you *do* imagine something with a mirror standing vertically in the middle of it, because you imagine something *more symmetrical than a human*. And so he *did* look like an alien. Like something not human.

Because what looks human about you is that the mirror in the middle of you is not really mirror. It is water.

It started as a family joke. Habit. A *tic*. Later it became a little more serious. After my bar mitzvah party he took me out to *Burger Ranch* in Haifa and said, 'You know, there's a lot to it, to the alien thing in the mirror. I gave it to you in the form of parable,' and I said, 'Sure, dad.' I thought knew. What *could* it mean? The only alien is *in you* or something. In your fear. Whatever. But as time passed he went on and on about the alien. He wrote *Symmetry: A Mind Virus* but no publisher wanted to print it. He kept talking about the alien long after I was too old to be afraid of aliens or cared to hear about them. When I was 15 he started losing his mind every time he went to work. He hated teaching. It didn't leave him enough time to write. He blamed the job for the failure of his book. At night I would hear him cry to my mom, like, 'I have so much to say, I have so much to say.' But even when he

111

did quit, no one published him until he started his own publishing house and published himself. By then I was 16 and dating Tania and already pretty far from faith. At first he didn't think it was serious. He said, 'The God you don't believe in? I don't believe in It either.' When he finally understood I just didn't care, it crushed him. It was so painful that he began to lose his own faith. Which of course made me doubt the strength of his faith to begin with, and so caused me to lose mine even more, and so on and so on. We had tonnes of fights about keeping Shabbat. You know how hard it is to not smoke or listen to music for a whole day and then convince yourself that *this* day is sacred? The *jail*-day?

You've got it all wrong. It's a day free of want. Want is the real jail.

Aren't they both jails?

They are. But one has no walls.

Six years after I moved to New York, he came to visit me. I wasn't in the best place in my life. Mora had just left me, and I couldn't afford rent, and I had to finish the mastering on the recordings, which I couldn't afford. So I started au pairing for the Rosens on Devoe street. They were this rich couple. She was a vet and he an architect and vice versa, and they had —

Do rich people live on Devoe Street?

Rich *for me*. They had a five-year-old daughter, Shir, and wanted a live-in au pair. So I got to live in their basement, which was cool because I didn't have to pay rent or buy food or drive to work, *and* I got paid, *and* I had a whole floor for myself where I could work on my music on my gear during the day when Shir was at school — *What*?

I didn't say anything.

Then I got pneumonia. The fact that I couldn't see a doctor because I didn't have health insurance wasn't so bad, but I was kind of confined to the basement. I didn't want Shir to get sick too, so I stayed down there for two weeks. During that time, I listened to the album I was working on over and over, trying to figure out how to master it. While listening, lyrics started popping into my head. Words just appeared on top of the melody. And the album, which was completely instrumental before, became an album of songs. I was so sick, all I could do was sing. And in English, so it took me a while to understand what I was singing about. I sang about things I didn't even think about. Apocalypse. The end of the world.

Yes.

The Rosens decorated the fence for Christmas even though they were Jewish, and I could see the fence from where I worked in the basement. I remember sitting there, working, listening to my own beats for the millionth time, totally sick, and suddenly getting drunk on nothing. Drunk on some sort of weird sense of victory. Like I was a general at the end of a war, and my army had won. As if I were at the finally silent battlefront, at the edge of the sea. Watching the last whispers of fire on the dark water, in the evening. The great sinking ships of my enemies.

Sinking or not, they are comfortable. You will never be comfortable.

Then I got better and my father flew over. I came to the airport to pick him up. When he stepped through the entrance gate he hugged and kissed me, but he looked pale. Terrified. In the taxi I asked him what was wrong, and he said, 'It's here. The alien is here.' I tried to keep up with the joke, so I said, 'I thought it was in your bedroom mirror.' He didn't think it was funny. He looked scared as shit. He said, 'But here it's *all around*.' Then he remembered that he'd brought me a present, dug around in his bag and gave it to me. It was an old Sandisk MP3 player. I told him my cell phone plays MP3s, so I didn't really need it, and that I'd upload songs on it for him so he could use it instead.

Don't touch your face. It's a Water Mirror coming out of your body to your eye in order to create small infinities of light straight into the retina. It's good.

I sublet a room for us on Driggs. We went to parks and museums. It was freezing cold. Everybody started saying 'selfie' all of a sudden. Everyone in New York was taking pictures of themselves with their phones. My father couldn't stop pointing at them. In restaurants, on the street. 'Look, there's another one!' he'd say, and I'd have to push his arm down and be like: 'Shhh, stop it.' I spent a whole day uploading songs on his MP3 player, but when I gave it to him he said he'd listen to it on the plane. He wanted to talk. He bought me lunch and asked: 'Do the Rosens know how old you are?' I said, 'No. I told them I was 23.' He asked me why, and I said, 'Because I look 23!' 'But why did you lie?' he asked. 'They're 31,' I said. '*I* can bear the fact that I'm only three years younger than them, and by the time I'm their age there is no way I will have their car or house or clothes or career or family or anything. But I don't think *they* can.' My father stopped eating. 'Are you protecting *everyone*?' he asked. And I said, 'Yes. Do you have a problem with that?' He said, 'On the plane ride here, they showed us a movie about emergency procedures. And they said in case of a drop in oxygen in the cabin, one has to put an oxygen mask on oneself before helping one's child do the same. One has to save oneself first. Otherwise one might actually kill both oneself and those one is trying to save, or at least allow them to be saved by a dead man.' I said, 'They said all that? Really?' Later, back at the apartment, I was taking a shit and I could hear him pacing by the door. I couldn't take it after a while, so I said, 'What the fuck, dad?' He stopped right in front of the door and said: 'You are not an artist. You don't even know how to digest *food*,' and I said, through the door, 'What did you just say?' and he said, 'You'd rather *shit* than *eat*. You'd rather give than take. But if you don't eat, what is it that you are shitting? Nothing. You are laying more and more layers of nothings where there should be *something*. Where you should be creating something out of nothing. Where you should be sucking shit through your bodies, and puking it out of your mouths as beautiful, nutritious food.' I was just having a terrible constipation so it was hilarious on many levels.

I would have thought he'd be a little harsher regarding your lifestyle. You try hard to portray him as a poor teacher, but in the last 11 years of his life, he was a pretty respected rabbi, and your life —

— Of course he wanted me to take over the publishing house. He said I could learn how to run a business this way, so later I could open my own *label* and publish my own music, like he did with his writing. I said something like, 'Who taught you how to say 'label'?'

Ha.

He said, 'Who taught you how to say 'who'?'

Right. Right.

On his last day in New York we got into a fight. We were walking to a subway station near Bryant Park, and we passed an Arab homeless woman with a child. I gave her a dollar. My dad shook his head, like he was deeply disappointed in me. I asked him what his problem was, and he didn't answer. I said, 'What, because they're Arab?' and he said, 'No.' I told him, 'You never give money to anyone,' and he went: 'I only give money to street performers.' He said it like it was a mitzvah only he was aware of: 'I only give money to people who *do* something.' A couple of minutes later we came across another homeless person. He was sitting on a wheelchair, covered in rags, and he didn't have any legs or hands. Just a head. We took the train home in silence. At dinner my father looked depressed. I asked him, 'Are you sorry you didn't give *him* money?' And he said, 'No.' I said, "What did you want him to *do*? Play the harmonica, hands-free, like Dylan?' And you know what he said? He said, 'He could still *sing*.' I got so pissed off I told him I was going out. I needed a drink. It was his last night, and I knew he was hoping we'd sit down and talk. He wanted to show me the last draft of the Second Book.

The Second Book was dedicated to you.

I leafed through the first. It seemed mad. It was the same mystical religious bullshit that got him excommunicated from *Beit Malka*.

It was all true.

You know its Gnostic thought, right? That it is *forbidden*?

No no no no no. Not if you know the mirror is also made of light. Not if it's built by human want. You think I am not made of the same infinite materiel that made you or wa —

Anyway I didn't want to hear about it, but when I was at the door he said, 'Can I come with you?' I acted like I didn't hear him and left, thinking he wouldn't follow because he didn't have his coat on, but he ran after me in the snow with just his sweater on. We walked down Metropolitan not saying a word until we got to Legion. It was too freezing to think. We got in, sat at the bar, got beers. He noticed this girl in the other corner of the room and went, 'Go talk to her!' I told him that the fact that he married mom when he was practically a baby didn't mean he now had to fuck the rest of the world by proxy via his offsprings. He didn't listen to me because he was staring at her body while she was dancing. I didn't feel like sitting next to a religious 60-year-old drooling at the bar, so I got up and went over to her. She stopped dancing and sat down. We spoke for five minutes. She was cute. I can't remember her name. Becca. After five minutes, my dad showed up and crammed in next to us. It was so embarrassing I had to act as though it was quirky and funny. Obviously I joked about him in English in front of her. He didn't speak any English, so he just listened and smiled like an idiot while I told her what he believes in. Then we went out to smoke and he came out with us and asked for a puff. I don't even think he knew it was weed. Later, when Becca was speaking about her friend who had to drive to work for two hours every day, she said, 'So every morning she commutes — ' and my father just burst out laughing. I'm talking beer out his nose all over the table, unable

to speak. I tried to calm him down, or at least to understand what had happened — like, 'Dad, what are you *doing*?' — and finally, when he caught his breath, he said, '*Commutes!*' and cracked up again. I said, 'What about it?' and he said, 'Is there really such a *thing*?' And I said, '*Commutes*? Of course, it means — ' And he said, 'No no no! Don't tell me what it means! It'll only ruin it!'

Wonderful.

But then something happened. We went back in, and suddenly this Becca goes, 'Wait a minute, how do you spell your last name?' B-A-R-S-K-I. Why? She put her left arm around me, and with her right hand, lifted her iPhone in front of us and took a picture. I stood there, watching, as she uploaded it on Facebook and tagged me. On the way home, my father asked me to explain what happened. I told him she had to take a picture of me and post it online so in case I have a girlfriend, my girlfriend would see it. And also in case anybody else she knows had anything to say about me, they could let her know. He thought about it for a long time. Then he looked at me and said, 'Are you what comes after human?' And I laughed and said, 'How do you mean?' And he said, 'Have you moved to Higher Mind?'

Like, the internet?

I don't know. I — Maybe like the cell phone is the new reflection of Self. The webcam is the first mirror in which our eyes don't meet their own reflection. Where the image is not created through the infinite loop of light. That is why we look completely different in every picture. But these images are then shared online into the larger mind of the internet where they are viewed by many people, perceived by many intelligences, and therefore receive their Infinite, ever-changing, Water-like-reflection dimension.

The Water Age is returning. It has been prophesised. Aharit Hayamim doesn't only mean 'End of Days' — it also means 'The Return of the Seas.'

Or it's just another mirror. Because the internet is built through our minds — which are already infested by you — so it too has a mirror in the middle of it. Now we can either use it to venture into further infinity by viewing the contents of each other's minds — all the art and libraries and diaries of the world are finally exposed — or we can use it to spiral into deeper solitude.

Like porn?

So is the iPad the 'Mirror Which Does Light' they were speaking about?

The Mirror Which Does —

You know, the mirror from Maimonides, the Maharal, the Shelah HaKadosh, the Malbim, when they speak about, 'All prophets prophesised in a Mirror Which Does Not Light but Moses prophesised in a Mirror Which Does Light.' Do you think it could be the iPad? I mean, the cellphone camera?

I didn't think about it. I need to think about that.

I will go blind if I don't blink soon.

Go.

Yeah?

Go, go. Dinner's on in about five minutes anyway.

I look stoned. I need to cover you up.

Natan?

What?

I love you.

NAMELESS AND SHAMELESS

LOIS H. GRESH

Lot scanned the Help Wanted ads nailed to the sign pointing to Ur. At 28, he had plenty of skills and could fill any number of these jobs. Jeroham-Shlem, the Overseer of Affairs, needed a courier to deliver mail between Ur and Babylon. For only one seah of barley for a day's donkey rental, Lot could get an animal from Uriel-Shub the Donkey-Man by the East Gate. This would make the courier job a snap.

'What do you think, Uncle Abe?'

'You can't leave home.' Abe stroked his matted, grey beard, which hung to his waist. 'Babylon can wait. I need you here. It's important. It's a mission from —' and he mumbled a word that sounded like Adonai.

Unfortunately for Lot, it had to be his uncle who was crazy, his uncle who started this whole 'one God' business, his uncle who smashed idols and raised all kinds of hell. Abe had to be there every Wednesday for the camel rodeo, didn't he? Had to be the best rider, had to push his camel to try and throw him. The old man rode animals so fast, Jeroham-Shlem had instituted a camel speed limit all around the outskirts of Sodom.

'What's so important that it can't wait a few months?' asked Lot. He settled on the rock next to his uncle and stretched his legs under the sun. The warmth made him woozy. He wished he could sip some fermented juice, but ever since Abe got on this 'one God' kick, Lot was only allowed the fermented juice once or twice a year. Lot wondered if his uncle was secretly a wino.

Abe lifted an arm and pointed toward the sand dunes and cliffs behind the tent. His eyes watered, maybe from drinking, maybe from senility — well, he was 99 years old — or maybe from the sun. 'They're coming from yonder hills, Lot, three tall strangers, and they've come to warn us.'

'I'm tired of all this, Uncle Abe. I need something different to do with my life. We can't all be you.'

His uncle frowned, and a pang of guilt swept through Lot followed by a wave of shame.

'You have news of Sodom, I take it?' Uncle Abe asked. Startled, Lot looked up to see three creatures squatting by the tent opening. He hadn't seen them come from any direction — had they simply sprung to life right here in the sand?

From his uncle's tone, it seemed that Abe already knew these three... men.

The furriest of them, the one with the extra-wide jawbones and the largest nostrils, grunted and said, 'News? The only news out of Sodom is that it's filled with freaks. Do you think our parents' parents' parents looked like us? God rest their souls, Hayim ben Saul ben Shmuel ben Yakov ben Hyksos.' He wore a loincloth that did little to hide his fur, his muscles, and the fact that his hands lacked thumbs and his feet lacked big toes.

The skinniest of the men, the one with the long nose and three eyes, said, 'I see no good coming of this, Abe. We barely got out of there alive, and look what it did to us. You should see what they're like back there.' He wore a black robe with a hood, and Lot wondered if he also had fur, no thumbs, and no big toes.

Perched high on the mountain overlooking Sodom, Lot had a clear view of the city. Even beneath the blaze of sun, Sodom sparkled like ten thousand jewels. Spires rose along the clay-stone walls, which according to Uncle Abe, were 24 cubits thick. The people of Sodom shrieked and laughed constantly, their voices a blanket of noise to the tent-dwelling families on the mount. In fact, the shrieks and laughter from Sodom went on all night and never stopped.

Lot recognized the third man. He was Litvin the Barbarian, protector of the Hyksos in all these parts. He stood six cubits tall. He carried a club with spikes sticking out of it in all directions. His arm was wider than Lot's torso. With a flick of his little finger, Litvin could easily snap Lot's neck, but they'd grown up together in the desert and Lot wasn't afraid of him.

The Barbarian spoke to his black-robed friend. 'Eliezer, Oh Prophet of Damascus, do you foresee anything good in our future?' His words were eloquent. Despite the fact that he was a near-naked giant wearing a scrap of camel hide to protect his privates, Litvin was highly educated.

Eliezer lifted both arms towards the heavens and intoned, 'Abram, true believer of the one —' he mumbled a word that vaguely sounded like Adonai — 'I've come to tell you that Sodom is doomed.' Beneath the black hood, his eyes glazed. A drop of moisture slinked from his lips. 'I have seen visions that give me no rest. Sodom is filled with debauchery that turns people into monsters as if born from some other place, far far away beyond the stars. Bordellos filled with madams and idolators, the slaying of innocents, the worship of chopped livers and pickled tongues. I tell you, these people are insane. They fight all night about Seth and Horus, and they hack each other to death and set themselves on fire.'

'But,' Lot interjected in a soft voice, 'what have you come to prophesise to us? Aren't all these things going on right now before our very eyes?'

'Yes, but I have Litvin with me for a reason. You see —' Eliezer trembled, then clutched his chest. He staggered and Lot eased him to a rock, where he sat and collected his wits.

Uncle Abe certainly had weird friends; but then again, thought Lot, what would you expect from a 99-year-old hell-raising idol-smashing camel-rodeo wino?

'Listen,' said Abe, 'the Prophet Eliezer has been telling me for weeks that Adonai is going to wipe out Sodom with violent winds, hailstorms, fire blasts from the sky, sulphuric flames shooting from the earth, and if you thought the Ark flood was bad, there's going to be a flood here, too, and it's going to be a killer —

Eliezer's voice rose to a wail, '— hail and fire and sulphuric flames and floods! And the almighty Adonai will split the earth in quake after quake and consume every man, woman, and child, every insectoid and tentacled nail creature in Sodom! I have seen it, and it will be so. Tonight.' He sank back, as if exhausted, and shut his eyes. Prophesizing must be exhausting work, thought Lot.

'Get my staff,' said Uncle Abe. 'Lot, you take Litvin and go to Sodom. Destroy whatever's taken over the city, causing Adonai such headaches. I want you to kill it. Do you understand?'

'Kill?' said Lot. 'Are you serious?'

'Very,' said Abe. 'If there are a hundred innocent people in there, get them out before the place blows.'

'And if there are only fifty?'

'Well, get them out.'

Eliezer piped up. 'You may not find even one innocent, ethical, moral person in all of Sodom.'

'Not even a baby?' asked Lot.

123

'Even their babies are corrupt,' said Eliezer.

Lot had his doubts, but he always did what Uncle Abe told him to do. So he let his wife know that he wouldn't be home that night and he set off with Litvin down the hill towards Sodom. Lot had a few weapons on him. He had Uncle Abe's staff as well as a slingshot and spear. Litvin the Barbarian had so many weapons strapped to his body that Lot didn't bother to tally them. He knew that, in the end, all Litvin needed was his physical strength.

At the city gates, two guards stopped Lot and Litvin and asked to see identification tattoos. Lot was mesmerised by their faces, or rather, lack of faces. Litvin smashed a club into what passed for voice holes surrounded by red fur, and both guards went down, their shrieks fading into the general Sodomic racket. Tentacles flailed, then twitched, then stopped. Lot and Litvin stepped over fleshy tumours and tentacles splayed like tangled hair across the sand.

All was mayhem in Sodom. Naked people shouted obscenities and dashed from shop to shop. Vendors raced after them, demanding payment. Camels reared up and crushed people beneath their hooves. A herd of donkeys riding camels riding gigantic formless creatures zipped past Lot on slate-like rollers.

Lot didn't know where to start the attack. How could they find whatever was causing the Sodomic calamities and stop it before tonight? It seemed impossible.

A half-female thing, part human and part rodent, threw herself at Litvin. Something jerked Lot's arm and a weasel the size of a small child ran into the throng of merrymakers, and with it went Uncle Abe's staff.

Lot was about to dash after the thief when Litvin tossed the human-rodent into a pile of scarves, paused, squinted, and said, 'Lot, isn't that your wife?'

'Excuse me?'

Litvin pointed a finger with more muscles in it than Lot had in his right arm. 'Over there, buying scarves, I think.'

Lot peered past the green men dotted with pock marks. Hair the colour of fire and eyes like almonds: his wife. She looped a shimmering scarf over her shoulders and swivelled, admiring the way the fabric clung to her curves.

What in the name of the nameless Almighty One was she doing here?

He shoved his way past the pock-marked creatures and grabbed his wife — she who had never been named by her parents, though Lot and Abram had often considered calling her Sheba or Edith. 'What are you doing? Go back to the tent!'

She pouted. 'I won't. I slipped in after you, and I'm staying. Why should you have all the fun?'

'You call this fun? Are you crazy?'

She took his hand and made him fondle the scarf draped over her chest. She was a handful, Lot had to admit, and this had been one reason he'd married her. There weren't many feisty girls among the tent-dwellers. Because his wife had no given name, when they made love, Lot sometimes screamed Osiris, which would wake up Abe, and the old man would start screaming about idols and shaking his fists.

Was that a tentacle he saw growing on her neck? He moved closer and gently touched her. Yes, it was a small growth, as long as a fingernail and as wide as a vein. He pulled back, and clenched his fists. Then he ripped the alien scarf off his wife, spun her around, and shoved her toward the gates of Sodom. 'Get out of here. I'm telling you, this place is going to blow! Go home!'

'No!' She struggled in his grasp, squirmed to get free, beat him with her fists. Crying now, begging to stay and watch the orgies over there, past the stalls of tref, the pig's feet and cheesy meats and lamb cooked in mother's milk.

Lot didn't have time for his wife's nonsense. He drew his spear. 'Go! I won't argue with thee, woman!'

She knew he meant business. He referred to her as 'thee' only when he was furious. She gasped, eyes wide, then ran into the crowd toward the city gates. Lot could only hope she would do as he said, go back to the tent where it was safe with Abram and protect their daughters.

Meanwhile, he had work to do with Litvin, who was battling several insectoids twice his height and four times his width. Lot drove his spear into one of the creatures, and blood the colour of the night sky spilled out. He grabbed the spear with both hands and yanked it from the thick hide, then drove it back into the creature, which squealed and spun black threads around Lot's body, no doubt trying to pin his arms to his sides. Overhead, the sky shook. Beneath him, the ground trembled. He could feel it: time was running out.

Lot leapt into the air, raised both of his feet and slammed them into the creature where its many legs sprouted from its flabby midriff. The thing staggered back, midriff jiggling, and a keening rose around Lot as a multitude of things closed in on him, angry.

Litvin was hacking at the creatures with his weapons — Lot saw blades and saws and clubs of all dimensions — and he lifted one by the throat and threw it into a group of goat-humans wrestling in a pit of wet sand. The girls, as Lot assumed they were from their slinky garments, bleated and scrambled on all fours from the pit, back hooves slipping, front hooves wrenching them up.

Litvin's creature landed with a loud thud and squealed. Geysers of wet sand erupted from the pit and doused dozens of goat-men waving money and hollering bets. Uncle Abe's friend was right. Sodom was a hell hole.

But Lot didn't have time to think past the simple conclusion that Eliezer was right, that even their babies were probably corrupt. His spear broke in the paws of a Sodomic male, and in that moment, Litvin the Barbarian raced head-first into the beast and slammed his skull into its rightmost arm. Two paws opened and six remained closed, but the two that opened dropped Lot's broken spear. Litvin's head was thicker than a boulder, and his aim was dead on.

As the Sodomites paused, apparently stunned that a mere human could fight them, Lot and Litvin dashed down the road and ducked behind a stall of fermented cactus fruits. They knocked the owner aside, and in a tangle of horns and nostrils and hair, the thing fell to the sand, clutching a fruit. Breathing heavily, Lot and Litvin pulled open a door behind the stall and slipped into a dark building made from hardened clay. The noise was less fierce inside, a relief.

'What causes such madness?' Litvin wiped the sweat from his eyes. 'Where do you think those creatures come from?'

Lot considered. Of all the things in this world without names, the creatures of Sodom were the strangest. He'd always thought Uncle Abe was weird. He'd always wanted to leave the tribe and live in a big city, maybe Babylon. Now, he wasn't so sure. Maybe Uncle Abe was the sane one, and maybe big city life wasn't all it was cracked up to be.

'I don't know where the Sodomites come from,' he said. 'Perhaps they come from afar, the other side of the sky or the depths of the ocean. Or perhaps they come when people worship idols. Perhaps Uncle Abe knows what he's doing.'

At that moment, the door opened and slammed against the wall, and light shot through the darkness. Something reeking of overripe cactus fruits staggered inside, leaned over, and thrust twelve horns into the hallway.

'The owner of the stall,' whispered Lot.

Litvin gestured towards the rear of the building. Lot nodded, yes, and followed Litvin down the hall, clutching at mud walls caked in slime. The cactus owner grunted, and as Lot and Litvin rounded one corner and then another, Lot heard its horns raking the walls farther and farther behind them.

It was hard for Lot to see anything. He groped his way along the walls, continuing to follow Litvin. The Sodomic noise grew dimmer, and the air grew thick and rank with mould laced with the sting of salt. Mice skittered underfoot.

Suddenly, Litvin paused, holding both arms out to block Lot.

'What is it?' whispered Lot.

'Stairs. They lead down. You game, or should I go alone?'

'Well, I'm not going to stay here alone,' said Lot. 'So I guess I'm coming along.'

'Then be careful.'

'Obviously. Come on, let's go, Shmuel, before that horned guy catches up.'

Litvin bristled. 'Don't ever call me that.'

'Then don't call me a wuss,' said Lot.

Litvin's given name was Shmuel Litvin ben Shlomo ben Shmuel ben Shneur ben Shmuel. Lot only used it when Litvin insulted his intelligence or physical prowess.

'Fine. So I was worried about you. Big deal. Listen, we're wasting time.' Litvin gripped both sides of the staircase and started his descent.

They moved slowly, unable to see anything in the dark. Down, down they went, deeper and deeper beneath Sodom. Lot must have counted two hundreds stairs, maybe more, before they reached bottom and the stairs gave way to uneven floor.

The salty odour grew as the mould subsided. Their feet crunched over what felt like tiny rocks. Must be salt, thought Lot. The walls were coated with the stuff and rough beneath his fingers.

The passageway narrowed, and the ceiling shrank down, lower and lower. They were in a tunnel made entirely of salt. Lot got on his hands and knees, crawling behind Litvin.

Jagged salt formations jutted from the floor and walls, and cut into his flesh. What was a little blood, a tiny sting, a gash here and there? Lot had endured much worse. He crawled on, ignoring the pain.

Finally, light filtered into the tunnel from ahead and cast green whorls upon the salt, which sparkled everywhere with an eerie sheen. The tunnel opened into a cavern.

Litvin scrabbled to his feet and looked around him with a stunned expression. Lot stood, and he couldn't help himself: he gasped.

On the cavern walls, green lanterns illuminated paintings of Sodomic creatures. The furniture was strange, nothing like city furniture, much less the boulders of Uncle Abe's tribe. Built from salt and unknown glowing materials, the chairs were tiny, stood on eight legs, and were curved to hold what Lot could only think of as spheres, and in some cases, bizarre geometric shapes for which — no surprise here — Lot had no names. Miniature tables held metal cylinders and boxes made from bark-like material.

The ceiling, a domed lattice, was as high as the mountains where the goats grazed. Cables and metallic objects dangled from the lattice grids.

Litvin the Barbarian smashed his club into one of the tables, which splintered and broke. He then smashed a metal cylinder, which oozed purple across the salt floor. The two men stared at each other for a moment, then Litvin raced to a tunnel on the cavern's left side and slipped into it. Lot followed and they squeezed through the tunnel, which twisted left then right then left again; and then dipped down, up, and now down again. An awful smell, like that of rotten eggs, filled the air. By the time they reached the tunnel's end, Lot's eyes burned with salt and his hair was encrusted with it, but he barely noticed. He was here to kill whatever had taken over Sodom. He was here on official business, that of Abe and Adonai.

He still didn't know how they were going to do it. Litvin was good at hand-to-hand combat. He could slay dozens of Sodomites within minutes. But Litvin couldn't take on thousands of them at once and shut down the city.

'What do you think we should do?' said Litvin.

Lot peered around the cavern, which was illuminated by torches and as big as Sodom itself. Like desert dunes, mounds of yellow rock stretched across the floor as far as Lot could see. Weird metal contraptions hulked along the walls like sleeping beasts, their limbs stretching into the ceiling and beyond.

Suddenly, Lot understood. A glimmer of comprehension, really, not the full meaning of the Sodomites, where they came from, who they were and what they wanted with humans. But he understood enough to know what he and Litvin had to do. 'We're looking at something not of this world,' he said. 'The wild and lascivious creatures of Sodom aren't human. They're of another time and place.'

'Perhaps from the stars?'

'Perhaps. I believe this yellow rock is what got them here, and these giant metal contraptions, they are clearly alien.'

He remembered Uncle Abe's words: 'If there are a hundred innocent people in there, get them out before the place blows.'

Before the place blows.

And the prophet Eliezer had insisted, 'You may not find even one innocent, ethical, moral person in all of Sodom.'

Eliezer was never wrong. Never. And this time it was because there were no people in Sodom.

'Shove the yellow rocks into the metal things,' Lot said.

Litvin nodded, apparently guessing what Lot wanted to do. They were going to blow this joint straight to the heavens.

With Litvin's muscles, it didn't take long to fill twenty of the metal contraptions with rock. Then, racing through the cavern, Lot and Litvin snatched torches from the walls and threw them into the contraptions.

'Run!' yelled Lot.

But he didn't need to tell Litvin to run, because the other man was already half-squeezed into the tunnel leading out.

Blue fire flamed behind them. The yellow rock melted into a blood-red ooze. Lot held his breath, as the rotten smell intensified in billows of blue smoke.

Chased by roiling malodorous smoke, they raced through the underground maze as quickly as they could. They slammed from the door into the streets of Sodom, smoke lacing the air, lashing the creatures like whips. All around them, the alien Sodomites shrieked with glee, ate tref tentacles, drank goat's milk with lamb's meat, and rolled together in the sand. They were still making merry, oblivious to their impending doom.

Many minutes later, far outside the city and high on the mountain, Litvin stood with his feet wide apart and his hands on his waist. Lot sank to a boulder, panting.

And now a boom!

Lot looked up. Then he slowly rose, barely able to grasp what he was seeing.

Fireballs blasted from Sodom, sending mud buildings into the sky along with green flesh and fat. The beasts shrieked, this time in pain as their bodies exploded to bits. Blue smoke billowed high into the clouds, and then a tidal wave of blood-red liquid rose from the edge of the city and crashed down. As the wave hit the ground and as the buildings smashed down, a violent wind shook the mountain, and then the sky opened and hurled balls of ice upon the ruins of Sodom.

About halfway up the mountain, Lot's wife staggered in blue smoke, dozens of alien scarves wrapped around her neck and body. She gestured wildly and screamed something that Lot couldn't hear, then turned; and a blast of blue hit her and receded, rolling back down the hill.

His wife — his nameless wife — stood like a salt statue, but only for a moment, and then she crumbled to dust.

It couldn't be, and why had she remained behind for so long? Why hadn't she listened to Lot when he told her to hurry back to Abe's tent? Why had she stayed for a pile of scarves? Or had she wanted more from life? Perhaps the allure of Sodom and its debauchery was too much for his poor tent-dwelling wife to resist. After all, Lot had always dreamed of finding himself and feeling free in Babylon or Ur.

Lot cried out, but Litvin grabbed his arm and wouldn't let him run down the incline. 'It's too late,' he said. 'Let it be — there's nothing you can do.'

And so it was, for the city of Sodom caved in, just sank into itself, it seemed, and a wash of water gurgled and then flooded the deep crater Sodom left behind. Quakes, floods, flames, hail, fire, smoke, the death of all aliens.

It was as Uncle Abe and Eliezer predicted.

This Adonai was powerful and not to be messed with.

By the pile of dust that had been his wife was the sign pointing to Ur. It creaked and wobbled, and as it fell, a blast of wind ripped off the Help Wanted ads, which disappeared into a cloud of alien smoke.

THE GHETTO

MATTHUE ROTH

For the longest time, Reb Chaim never got sick. When people asked him how, he said he did it so that he could serve G-d with all his faculties, that there was nothing worse than a half-done job. 'No, really,' they'd say, 'what's your secret?' There were a thousand things it could have been. He woke every day between four and six, always an hour before sunrise. He never ate in restaurants, and he cooked all his own food — his wife used to, but Henya got hit with arthritis when she turned 60, and he liked cooking better than she did, anyway. 'No secret,' he would say. 'I just got a good deal with G-d. Hashem takes care of me, and I take care of Hashem.'

Then one day, Reb Chaim's rabbi, Rabbi Danzig, suggested to him that maybe he should reconsider. 'After all,' he said, 'you have six grandchildren living in your home, and two dozen others stop by every day to visit. Who are you to deprive them of the commandment to visit the sick?'

Reb Chaim had never looked at it that way before. Still, something bothered him about the equation. 'They eat my food,' he protested. 'If I am sick, and I cannot cook, nobody will be able to make a blessing on my food. How many commandments will that deny the world?'

'Pride!' Rabbi Danzig shrilled at him. 'Excessive boastfulness! You think it's your cooking that keeps the world in motion? See what happens if you don't for a week make your miso vegetable soup. Commandments will still be obeyed. The sun will still rise in the morning.'

Rabbi Danzig's voice grew from shrilling to growling to a roaring inferno. Of all his students, of all the Jews in Crown Heights, Reb Chaim was one of the only ever to incur his full wrath. He held nothing back. In a way, it was a compliment. Embarrassing someone, in Torah law, was the equivalent of killing him or her. Over years, over decades, Rabbi Danzig and Reb Chaim had pushed each other to their respective limits, reduced each other to pure, holy nothingness, discovered new limits. So when Rabbi Danzig flew in Reb Chaim's face and insulted him, it was, in a way, a compliment.

Reb Chaim was thoughtful. 'Hmm,' he said. 'It's a good proposition.'

So the next week he fell sick. Nothing drastic, just a runny nose and some sporadic coughing. But because of his age, they didn't want it to grow into something bigger, so Chana, his oldest great-niece, made him

134

a bed on the living-room sofa, and kept a pot of fresh green tea by him so he could receive guests, but he still had his own semi-private bedroom to retreat to when he needed.

People came from all over Crown Heights, his students and friends, his relatives and in-laws, his former boarders, his future boarders. The house was packed; it was like a party. The walls swelled and stretched like the Leviathan-skin walls of the Great Sukkah, which the Talmud teaches will hold all the righteous during the destruction at the End of the World. They brought in a Torah and held morning prayers; they brought in pillows for Reb Chaim and prayed the evening service late at night, almost after midnight, when the gangs of cousins had finally trickled out from the place.

And yes, it was strange that Reb Chaim had a rabbi. Reb Chaim was, after all, the doyen of 770, the largest synagogue in Crown Heights, the regular reader of the Torah and the most prominent storyteller at the gatherings that followed services. He was as close to a de facto rabbi as that house of anarchy would ever get. But the Torah teaches: find yourself a rabbi to guide you and a student you can teach; and even Reb Chaim still had things to learn.

His rabbi, Rabbi Danzig, fulfilled the commandment of visiting Reb Chaim that Thursday morning. He prayed the afternoon prayers with the rest of the visitors, and in the wake of the group's dispersal, he took a private audience with Reb Chaim. The yeshiva boys around them spoke louder in deference to them, so nobody would appear to be eavesdropping.

'All right, all right,' said Rabbi Danzig. 'You've made your point to G-d; you've let many people wish you a speedy recovery.'

'Five hundred forty-three,' said Reb Chaim, brightly, but without a taste of pride. 'The cheder brought by the youngest classes today.'

'But it has got to stop,' Rabbi Danzig said. 'We all have our mission in this world, and it is time for you to get back to yours.'

Reb Chaim's marble-small eyes popped open, and his white tendrils of beard bobbed up and down. 'I will pray for it,' he said. 'I'll see what I can do.'

By Thursday afternoon he was walking about, and Thursday evening he had recovered almost entirely — and a good thing too, for it was almost Shabbos and they were way behind on cooking. Auntie Sima had started on the cholent, but then her arthritis flared up; Reb Chaim had gently tried to suggest to the boys staying in the spare bedroom that they might prepare the week's Sabbath dinner. They took it as a practical joke, Reb Chaim's sense of humour on the path to recovery. That's what he deserved for being so casual in his everyday speech. When he was a child, learning in the court of the Frierdiker Rebbe, school would let out early on Friday and he would go — both Reb Chaim and the Rebbe, that is — to prepare for the Sabbath. Today, these kids were accustomed to having all the real work done for them, no earthly concerns at all. Perhaps this was a blessing. This way they could study Torah till the very last moments before the sun went down and Sabbath set in.

And so, shortly after nightfall on Thursday night, Reb Chaim swung his feet to the ground for the first time that week. He called to Sima that he would be back shortly. He collected a handful from their stash of canvas grocery bags, and he set off to market.

Going out at night was not his first choice. He liked to be out early, catch the world by surprise. Already he was dreading the fruit bins filled with picked-over citrus and strawberries squashed between boxes. But what choice did he have? This was the hand G-d dealt him.

He also had to buy meat, which he could do in the Jewish area. For produce this late, however, there was only the supermarket, where everything was old and tasted like packing peanuts. It was also twice as expensive — as if anyone had heard of a kosher banana, a kosher butternut squash. What would people have done in Russia? Starved!

It was the kind of night that made you wary. Hot like day, but with a rumble in the air that gave you shivers. A gang of young black children scurried in front of him, brushing up close and knocking him halfway off the sidewalk. Insolent kids! He didn't hold it against them, but rather their parents, or whoever it was that raised them. In Crown Heights, his Crown Heights, kids were as rude as they came, but they respected their elders. He could ask a five-year-old great-grandson to buy a quart of milk, and the boy would, no questions asked. Not for Shabbos shopping, of course — this was too complicated — and he would never send them to this part of town, but there was an obeisance, an underlying morality, that these kids lacked. There was a sort of fear that normal people had, a holy fear, that nobody had ever taught them.

In the store were more black kids, a lot of them. Not buying anything, merely standing around. In the halogen glow it felt like midday. A lone fan blew uselessly, streaking a single trickle of air across the store. On the front door he had read a sign, hand-printed and misspelled, 'ON SCHOL OURS ONLY 2 CHILRUN IN SIDE AT 1 TIME'. What, he thought, about at eleven in the evening? How come the shopkeeper wasn't enforcing the rules he himself had laid out? He looked and learned why. The clerk was himself merely a teen, the minutest drizzle of facial hair only starting to blossom on his chin, no bigger than Reb Chaim's cheder nephews. The poor boy: forced to work this graveyard shift, kept up half the night.

That was the problem of coming here — outside the Jewish area, to a place that had no rules. They didn't have tradition to guide them, nor did American law hold any authority. Growing up without any rules of their own, how would they ever learn to respect anyone else's?

He brushed past the children to the tomatoes. They lay in a loose pyramid, stacked inside an upturned barrel, one of the shop's few concessions to fashionable design. It actually looked nice. He sorted through the offerings and found a dozen or so that weren't too hard or bruised. Then he turned to the lemons. The blessing of these long hot days was the multitude of ways to relieve oneself of the heat: turning on the air conditioning for an hour or drinking some cold lemonade. He would make a batch of lemonade for Shabbos, famously tart, and pour it into a cooler in the fridge. By Shabbos afternoon it would be wonderfully cool.

The lemons were a perfect ethereal yellow, like the golden cherubs in the Temple, like the sun itself. His thumb ran along the turf of skin, massaging the pores, testing its hardness. Behind the fruit's small pupik, he sensed another set of circles. He looked up into a pair of eyes, a child's: bright, supernaturally big, wild, dancing with intelligence.

'You got a problem?' the girl said when Reb Chaim noticed her.

'No problem,' said Reb Chaim. 'I am only searching for lemons.'

Instead of replying to him directly, the girl turned back over her shoulder, yelled to her flock of playmates. 'This cheap crazy Jew!' she said. 'He's hunting for the biggest lemons so he don't have to pay as much!'

His face burned. He didn't know whether to explain that, no matter what the size, harder lemons yielded more juice; or that lemons in this store were priced by weight, not quantity, and it didn't matter if he picked out the biggest lemon in the barrel, he'd still be charged more for it than a smaller lemon, and he was not in fact being a cheap Jew.

It was too late, though; her friends had assembled, all of them. They surrounded him, laughing like monkeys, one of them with a can of black beans in her hand, imitating his every movement with the lemon. She scrutinised the label. She weighed two cans of beans in her hand, one against the other. Others were laughing. One boy was doubled over. Another was bouncing up and down, shrieking out, 'He should shoplift them things in his beeerd!' and the rest of them howling in agreement.

A jolt of pain rocked his stomach. It embarrassed him that anyone would think these things, about him or any other Jew. He turned around. He tried to run away, but they were everywhere. He did a full-circle turn. Face-to-face with his original antagonist, he said: 'I would never! Stealing is against the Ten Commandments.' He thought that would help, drawing a bridge between their two religions.

Instead of helping, though, it only fed their spirits. They threw their heads back. Their mouths were wide, white, full of teeth. They rocked with laughter, laughter like an earthquake. 'You,' he growled. 'You paupers.'

Now, in Judaism, being poor is no great tragedy. Certainly it's better to be comfortable, or even rich — there's no commandment against indulging in the permitted luxuries of this world, such as fine food or a trip to Hawaii — but poverty is not a condition that should be disparaged. You can try to make money or you can go with the flow, but ultimately pay and poverty are both up to G-d.

Reb Chaim knew this, and he knew it better than most. At various points in his life, he'd been a successful businessman, investing in a Passover matzo factory that, due to a series of bizarre episodes one year, became unexpectedly the only operation in town whose supplies were unspoiled by a series of freak water leaks. And he's been basically a pauper himself, after the factory went broke and Reb Chaim was unable to find another job. He was too old to attend a kollel, and too learned in Talmud already. Not to say that he couldn't learn more — you can always learn more — but Reb Chaim was beyond that point in his life. He was too respected to do anything but be a rabbi, but he was too respected to be given anything but the highest rabbinical posts, and they were all filled.

Embarrassing someone was like killing them. Reb Chaim had been alive for 80 years, in Crown Heights for 69 of them — enough time to have been killed several times over — and in Russia before that. Most of his life in Russia, he couldn't remember. But he remembered this. His mother had taken him to the grocery store, unable to hold his hand because she feared dropping her food tickets, and so both her palms were stuffed tight with them. He had held onto the bottom hem of her coat. They stood waiting for hours, long enough for his skin to grow cold and then hot and then numb, a puffy and blustery shade of red. And then men came along. Younger than his mother, older than him. They shouted at them. They started pushing his mother. When little Reb Chaim wouldn't let go, they started on him. Calling him names. Saying things to him. He didn't understand what they were saying, or what these things meant, but he knew he was meant to be hurt.

He cried. The other people in line looked away from the pair, willing them to not exist. His mother picked him up, though he was too old to be carried, and she ran, all the way home, twelve long blocks. Maybe that was the first day he died. Or maybe it was only the first time he remembered. And now he had done the same thing. Half a world away, in another grocery store, he had committed murder.

Then he was falling. He was floating. He was a million miles away. He saw all the esoteric reasons for the irrational commandments they obeyed, listed like graffiti on a wall in front of him. He saw the winter constellations and the summer constellations at the same time, both sides of the sky like a giant sphere observed from the inside.

Now in front of him were Moses, David, the Baal Shem Tov — one a charlatan with a birth defect, born into a princehood he did not earn; one an abused shepherd, forced to run from his murderous brothers; one a teacher to the ignorant masses, who said that singing and dancing was more powerful than prayer, and was attacked by the leaders of the Jewish people, who made their money charging people for prayer. Their faces and bodies danced in the flames. They, too, were dying horrible deaths.

He zoomed back and he saw the whole of Earth, the whole history of humanity. Nations burning. People killing people. And behind it all, so faint that Reb Chaim could barely make them out at all, were the children from the store, the ones he'd so grievously wronged.

He twisted his head. He could barely move — it was like twisting through a block of Silly Putty. From the absolute corner of his eye, he could see the cashier, that boy, floating in the air, hovering above his register, his mouth wide open like he was screaming, no sound at all. Slowly but constantly, he was floating over the counter. Assembled around him in a loose circle were half a dozen tall, thin men. They all wore neat little grey suits. They were all bald.

They had big, prominent buggy eyes that seemed to eat up the whole room, yet saw nothing at all. It wasn't like they couldn't spot Reb Chaim and the children — it was more like, he felt, they just didn't care. Three or four of the men began to guide the cashier along, nudging him in the air like a giant balloon. One of the others tramped ahead. Two more came in their direction, one towards the children, one towards Reb Chaim. The man held up a small grey sphere. It was coated in the same colour as their uniforms. Already Reb Chaim could feel his memories peeling off like paper, flitting away on the night wind. The sickness that he'd let enter his body. His childhood, first in Vilnius, then the boat, then Brooklyn. His home and synagogue address. The first dinner he'd ever cooked his wife. The creature in front of him. The horrible embarrassment of the children and their laughter.

He stopped.

When you get older, your body betrays you. Certain things that used to work perfectly don't work any more. Your memories, which have always been stored in your brain like a well-ordered library are suddenly out of order, dust covers rearranged, pages swapped around, pages ripped out.

But there are certain things, other things, that you discover how to do, like muscles you've just used for the first time. You gain mastery over certain things — the chemicals, in your stomach and over your eyes, that do cleaning and digestion; how the wind smells before spring rain rushes in; the feeling of a lunatic moon; the involuntary spasms and knee-jerk reactions that your body was born with, that you, after 80 or so years, now can override. That was how Reb Chaim learned to make himself sick.

And that was how he grabbed onto his memories now: forced them back into his brain, yanked them with the utter force of his own belief, not because of any particular desire or melancholy but because he needed the embarrassment of being laughed at. It was a sign from G-d, a sign that he wasn't perfect yet. He still had things to work on. No one in Crown Heights — the Jewish Crown Heights, the proper Crown Heights — would ever dare laugh at Reb Chaim. And if he forgot what it was like, if he let the memory expire and float away, then he would have nothing. It would be like he'd never gotten that gift from G-d.

And he couldn't only keep his own memory of it, either. The children had to remember — of that, he was sure. Once the memories rushed back into his head, the creature stumbling toward him reeled back as if slapped, and the other creature, the one working on the children, was similarly shaken.

Reb Chaim used the last of his physical strength to hurl himself at the second creature. The first one was doing a good enough job on his own, shuddering wildly, collapsing against the ice-cream freezer. Both toppled over, and the memory device fell from the creature's hand.

The children shook themselves awake. They stared at each other, into one another's faces, as if relearning forgotten alphabets. Some of them walked over to the fallen creatures, prodded their unmoving bodies, retreating when they felt the soapy consistency of their skin. Then one of the kids looked at Reb Chaim and gave him a squinted-up face, as if trying to remember where she recognized his silvery mane.

Her attention was diverted by a scream from the door.

'They got Jesse!' she cried. 'They floatin' him away in the air!'

That was all the kids needed. They shook themselves into action, dashed through the door, screaming and fiery, in a stampeding pursuit of the creatures and their friend.

Reb Chaim walked to the door and leaned against its mezuzah-less frame. The metal was smooth, but he missed the feel of hard plastic jutting into his back — it had been ages since he'd stood in a doorway with no mezuzah. Out on the street, people were frozen in mid-walk, mid-conversation, mid-fight. The world was peaceful and still. Only the children from the store, the children who'd laughed at him (the children he saved, the thought sprung up in his mind, and was immediately banished) were in motion. They had found the grey men, and were presently engaged in jumping on them, beating them, tearing the creatures away from their friend, the boy at the cashier's booth. Perhaps Reb Chaim should tell them to go lightly. That the One Above punishes evildoers and those who deserve it; that it was not in our province to mete out justice without a fair trial.

But, no. He'd been a distinguished-looking old man for long enough. He knew that some lessons merely had to be learned in the doing.

Reb Chaim turned back to the produce carts. A few had been upended, but most were still in serviceable condition. He did a squat and sorted through a few of the lemons on the floor. A really good one brushed against his fingers, then rolled away into some unreachable crevice. It didn't matter. There were more than enough here.

When he had finished, the children were still not back. The two unconscious creatures who'd been on the floor were also gone — vanished, suddenly yet somehow unremarkably, each into a shimmer of pale blue. He counted out exact change from his wallet and left it on the cash register, obscured from potential thieves by a small bag of potato chips on top. He didn't have exact change: he was half a dollar over, which normally would cause him to stand in a corner of the store and wait, patiently but respectably, for another customer to materialise with sufficient funds for his reimbursement.

Tonight, he decided to leave it and head home.

'Chaim, what took you so long?' said his wife when he crept in. She was already in bed, but not yet asleep — Chaya had a terrible time letting herself go to sleep at night. His absence probably magnified her unease. She had the radio on, tuned to the news channel, which usually she wanted for white noise. Tonight, however, it was buzzing, the announcer talking rapidly and excitedly: strange lights seen over Brooklyn, low-flying planes. Reb Chaim rolled down the volume and, as unobtrusively as he could, switched it to the oldies station.

EXCISION

NAOMI ALDERMAN

Transcript from *In The Spirit*, a light-hearted weekly vidcast across the five systems on matters of faith, cultural spiritual practice, ancestor worship and the Quantum Gods.

Starts at 0012:38:92 of the programme.

…and on that subject, we're joined today from the gas planet Procyon 12 by an entity who's made quite the journey in spiritual outlook. N'kk'd>>f — I hope I'm pronouncing that correctly?

Not bad. Human tongues can't really manage the >>.

I'm embarrassed now I hear you pronounce it! Great! So, why don't you tell us what made you decide to convert to the Earth religion of 'Judaism'?

I've always been a searcher, I suppose. The values of Judaism appealed to me: a lot of emphasis is placed on the family. The peoples of Procyon 12 have rather complex families — each grouping contains four genders — so I was pleased to find a system of thought that put the family at the centre. And of course there was a more serious —

Right, right, amazing. Now my notes tell me that the leaders of this religion, the 'rabbis', tried to put you off?

That's right, Dirk. Judaism isn't a proselytising religion. They turned me away three times, according to their custom.

I'd think you might want to be put off, given that you have to have… is this right… they cut a bit off your sex organ when you join? That's a bit harsh, isn't it?

Ah, of course, yes, the circumcision process was quite problematic! I am of a gender unknown among humans. I have a protuberance with which I can begin the process of mate-impregnation, but when the act is complete the member breaks off and remains with my partner. A new member then grows within 72 hours. Well, it was faster when I was younger.

A...ha?

Yes, it was quite the conundrum for the rabbis! The sign is of a permanent covenant — but my sexual organs are extremely impermanent!

Sounds like a... puzzler?

Yes indeed. Well put. In the end, after some Talmudic discourse, it was decided that I could cut a permanent notch in my... ah, it is hard to describe in human terms. It is the frilly flesh-part which stands up on the back of my head when I am ready to mate.

Right! And are any of your other partners interested in joining you on your spiritual quest?

Not mine, no. Several friends have expressed an interest, but I believe I'm the first person on my planet to take the plunge, as it were.

To have the snip.

Quite.

Now, fitting a bi-gendered religion to a people with four genders. Tricky at all? I understand that the people of Procyon 12 fall into, basically, for the viewers, two different kinds of bloke and two different kinds of woman.

No, it would not be correct to call them two forms of male and two female, no. It is complex. These terms do not have the meaning for us that they have for you.

What would you call them, then?

The closest form is... you might call them right and left and up and down. And centre.

And centre?

Right and left and up and down and centre, yes.

That's... five.

Yes.

I thought you said there were four.

Yes. There are four.

So what's... centre?

Ah. We hope for their return.

We don't have much time, I'm afraid, N'kk'd>>f, so I'm going to ask you to tell me more — but briefly, if you could?

It is a matter of some shame to my people.

I'm sorry to hear that. But, briefly...

To create new life, four partners are needed. The first impregnates the second. The second hosts the foetus for three months before passing it on to the third, who adds certain DNA modifiers. The third hosts for another 21 days before passing to the fourth, who provides the amniotic sac and swaps in some RNA. After 36 days, the amniotic sac must be passed back to the first impregnator, who hosts the foetus to term — another eight months.

Fascinating. And complicated! Must take a lot of commitment.

This is why we place such emphasis on family.

And the... fifth gender?

We destroyed them.

Right.

They were not necessary to the process.

I see.

The rhetoric was that they were parasites. Their role was only to add certain DNA switching chemicals at the fifth and twenty-sixth week. They never hosted the foetus. It is history for us now. A politico-philosophical movement among my people 300 years ago declared them... lesser beings.

Right.

They contributed nothing, you see.

I'm being told we have to —

They were only a small fraction of us. Fewer than one per cent of births would belong to this fifth gender. We hunted them down. Where they were sheltered, we rooted them out. We knew them by the unusual colour of their eyes. By the lower tone of their voices. It took 100 years. And only then did we know that without their DNA-switching properties there would never be another of them.

And you —

It's not that they had a special power, or some innate ability. But we destroyed part of our own people. The body will never be whole again. There has been a great deal of regret among us for what we have done.

That's fascinating and tragic. Thank you, N'kk'd>>f, for —

This was what I saw among the Jewish people, you understand.

We have to —

I was only a youngster, 300 years ago. I didn't know what I was doing. But I suppose I... I suppose I've been searching for someone to forgive me.

Cut to commercial.

CONTRIBUTORS

ANDREA PHILLIPS is an award-winning writer and game designer who has worked on projects such as The Walk, Zombies, Run!, and The Daring Adventures of Captain Lucy Smokeheart. Her debut novel, *Revision*, will be out in spring 2015.

One of ROSANNE RABINOWITZ's first stories appeared in *The Slow Mirror: New Fiction by Jewish Writers*, but no extraterrestrials were involved. Her fiction has since found its way to places like *Postscripts*, *Midnight Street* and *Black Static*, and she completed a writing MA at Sheffield Hallam University. Her novella Helen's Story (PS Publishing) was shortlisted for the 2013 Shirley Jackson award. She has also contributed to anthologies such as *Rustblind and Silverbright, Never Again: Weird Fiction Against Racism and Fascism, Extended Play: the Elastic Book of Music, Mind Seed* and *Horror Uncut*. Her reviews and articles have appeared in Interzone and Paradox, and she contributes non-fiction to union, community and activist websites.

ERIC KAPLAN is a television writer and philosopher. He has worked for Futurama, Flight of the Conchords, The Simpsons and The Big Bang Theory where he is currently a co-executive producer. His book *Does Santa Exist: A Philosophical Investigation* was published by Dutton in 2014. His work is available at ericlinuskaplan.wordpress.com.

RACHEL SWIRSKY holds an MFA in fiction from the Iowa Writers Workshop where she wrote a bunch and learned about how to be very cold. She is now back in California where she lives in a desert and is learning about how to be quite hot. Her short fiction has appeared in numerous magazines and anthologies including Tor.com, Subterranean Magazine, and Clarkesworld, been nominated for several of the major science fiction awards, and won the Nebula Award twice. Her second collection, *How The World Became Quiet: Myths Of The Past, Present And Future*, came out from Subterranean Press in 2013.

JAY CASELBERG is an Australian author based in Europe, His work has appeared in many venues worldwide and his most recent novel,

Empties, is available now. He can be found at http://www.jaycaselberg. com

ELANA GOMEL is an Associate Professor at the Department of English and American Studies at Tel-Aviv University. She is the author of six non-fiction books and numerous articles on subjects such as postmodernism, narrative theory, science fiction, Dickens, and Victorian culture. Her latest books are *Narrative Space and Time: Representing Impossible Topologies in Literature* (Routledge 2014) and *Science Fiction, Alien Encounters, and the Ethics of Posthumanism: Beyond the Golden Rule* (Palgrave/Macmillan, 2014). Her fantasy stories appeared in New Horizons, Aoife's Kiss, Bewildering Stories, Timeless Tales and the anthologies *People of the Book* and *Dogstar and Other Science Fiction Stories*. She is also the author of a fantasy novel *A Tale of Three Cities* (Dark Quest Books, 2013).

GON BEN ARI is a writer, screenwriter and musician currently living in Brooklyn, NY. His feature film, Der Mensch, is a Yiddish-speaking Western now in pre-production with director Vania Heymann.

LOIS H. GRESH is the New York Times Best-Selling Author (6 times), Publishers Weekly Best-Selling Paperback Author, Publishers Weekly Best-Selling Paperback Children's Author, and USA Today Best-Selling Author of 27 books and 55 short stories. Current books are *Dark Fusions: Where Monsters Lurk!* (editor, PS Publishing, 2013), story collection *Eldritch Evolutions* (Chaosium 2011, BookViewCafe ebook 2012), and *The Divergent Companion* (St. Martin's Press, 2014). Anthology *Innsmouth Nightmares* (PS Publishing, 2015) is forthcoming. Lois has received Bram Stoker Award, Nebula Award, Theodore Sturgeon Award, and International Horror Guild Award nominations for her work.

MATTHUE ROTH is the author of *The Gobblings*, a children's book about a boy who saves a space station overrun by monsters, and the picture-book adaptation *My First Kafka*, and some other books that aren't for children. He lives in Brooklyn and keeps a secret diary at matthue.com.

NAOMI ALDERMAN is a novelist, broadcaster and games designer. She's won numerous awards for her literary novels which include Disobedience and The Liars' Gospel. She broadcasts regularly on BBC Radio 3 and Radio 4, and has a regular monthly column in the Observer. She is the co-creator of the hit smartphone fitness game Zombies, Run! In 2012 she was selected by Granta as one of their once-a-decade list of Best of Young British Novelists, and in 2013 she was picked for the Rolex Arts Initiative as the mentee of Margaret Atwood.

Mosac (British charity No: 1139077) provides practical and emotional support to non-abusing parents, carers and families of children who have been sexually abused.

The charity was formed in 1992 when four mothers whose children were abused came together and drew strength from each other's shared experience and realised the need for a similar service for others.

Based in Greenwich in south London, Mosac offers a national helpline, as well as counselling, advocacy, support groups and play therapy, and aims to break the silence surrounding child sexual abuse by raising awareness through training and consultancy.

Proceeds from the sale of this book will be donated to Mosac.

Made in the USA
Middletown, DE
03 February 2021